Christmas in the Harbour

Victoria Barbour

— HEART'S EASE, BOOK 6 —

FLANKER PRESS LIMITED
ST. JOHN'S

Library and Archives Canada Cataloguing in Publication

Barbour, Victoria
    Christmas in the Harbour

Issued in print and electronic formats.
ISBN 978-1-177117-440-4 (paperback).

A CIP catalogue record for this book is available from Library and Archives Canada.

© 2017 by Victoria Barbour

PRINTED IN CANADA

MIX
Paper from responsible sources
FSC
www.fsc.org   FSC® C016245

This paper has been certified to meet the environmental and social standards of the Forest Stewardship Council® (FSC®) and comes from responsibly managed forests, and verified recycled sources.

Cover Design by Crystal McLellan

FLANKER PRESS LTD.
PO BOX 2522, STATION C
ST. JOHN'S, NL
CANADA

TELEPHONE: (709) 739-4477   FAX: (709) 739-4420   TOLL-FREE: 1-866-739-4420
WWW.FLANKERPRESS.COM

9 8 7 6 5 4 3 2 1

We acknowledge the financial support of the Government of Canada through the Canada Book Fund (CBF) and the Government of Newfoundland and Labrador, Department of Tourism, Culture, Industry and Innovation for our publishing activities. We acknowledge the support of the Canada Council for the Arts, which last year invested $157 million to bring the arts to Canadians throughout the country. *Nous remercions le Conseil des arts du Canada de son soutien. L'an dernier, le Conseil a investi 157 millions de dollars pour mettre de l'art dans la vie des Canadiennes et des Canadiens de tout le pays.*

ALSO BY VICTORIA BARBOUR

Join Victoria's emailing list and never miss a new release. Plus, you'll get the first chance to review upcoming books for FREE! You can sign up on her website, www.victoriabarbour.com, or on her Facebook page: www.facebook.com/victoriabarbourromance.

Heart's Ease Series
Against Her Rules (Book 1)

Hard As Ice (Book 2)

Play Me (Book 3)

21st Century Rake (Book 4)

Wilful Desire (Book 5)

Christmas in the Harbour (Book 6)

Ida and the Nor'easter: A Heart's Ease Short Story

Forever Geek Trilogy
Geek God

Geek Groom

First Street Church Kindle World
Love's Atonement

DEDICATION

For everyone who chased me until I finished this story. And as always, to Reg and Rowan, for making it worth it.

In case you're wondering if you've read this before . . .

No. It's not déjà vu. There's a chance you may have read a version of this book in the past. *Christmas in the Harbour* began as a novella, and it ended once Hannah and Toby arrived in Heart's Ease. It was released as an ebook in late 2015. Since then, many, many readers have begged to know what happened once they got to Heart's Ease.

Thanks to Flanker Press, I've brought Hannah home for the holidays and have taken great pleasure in sharing some of my favourite things about a Newfoundland Christmas.

Plus, I have a surprise for you when you're done their story. Read to the end to find out!

Happy reading! And season's greetings, no matter what season you're in. Christmas books are good all year long!

— Victoria

ONE

∾

Her first mistake was watching *Man of Steel* before going to bed. There was something about Henry Cavill as a too-ripped-to-be-true fisherman that spoke to her inner bayman. Hannah liked her men big and beefy and hard-working. The thing about Superman was that he put all the real-life fishermen of Heart's Ease to shame. She knew it wasn't fair to compare real-life mortals to a superhero, but damn it all, once a gal saw Henry Cavill stomping around a small fishing village all wet and shirtless, well, there was no way to erase that from the pleasure bank that resided deep in her brain.

Hannah's second mistake was falling asleep on the sofa. Or, more specifically, falling asleep on the sofa wearing her roommate's hoodie. A hoodie that carried the sandalwood scent of the bane of Hannah's existence. Hannah Nolan loved to loathe Toby Sweeney. More to the point, she had to convince herself that she loathed him, because the other possibility was too much to bear: she loathed her love of him.

1

With these two missteps, was it any wonder that her dreams were plagued by equal parts erotic fantasy and tempestuous reality? As far as the face was concerned, it wasn't a stretch that Superman turned into Toby. They both had the same dark brown hair bordering on black. And then there were the eyes. The piercing, intense blue eyes that dared a woman to look away. But that's where the similarity ended. Toby wasn't a towering six-foot-plus mass of muscle. He was an average five eight, five nine? A decent body. Hell, you couldn't live with a guy and not see him shirtless or prancing around in boxer briefs from time to time. But he wasn't strapping and heroic, and he had no place in her dreams.

Try as she might, Hannah couldn't exorcise Toby from the lusty scene. So she did the only thing a girl who hasn't had sex in nearly six months could do. She settled in for the night and let Henry and Toby interchangeably have their nimble way with her.

In the gauzy wonderland of sleep, Toby had just started doing something wicked with his tongue. She'd made her peace with the notion that he couldn't keep out of her dream, and had learned that he was far more gifted in the arts of the bedroom than the man of steel. His tongue traced a path down her belly, and she tingled with the knowledge of where this was leading. Which is why it was puzzling to hear him speaking in her ear when his mouth was about three inches from heaven.

"Hannah, go up to bed."

"I am in bed," she muttered, slightly annoyed with him for speaking. Toby always ruined things when he talked.

"Come on. You'll be crooked in the morning if you don't move."

"Keep this up and I'm getting Henry back," she warned.

"Henry?"

"Shut up and get back to work," she said.

Now he was tugging at her hand. "I'm just home from work. Now get your arse up and go to bed."

Forcing her eyes open, she saw all too clearly. The dream was over. This wasn't the Toby of her dreams. It was the real one. The one who made every moment of her life a battle of wills.

"Why did you wake me?" she grumbled as she sat up.

"Because the last time I let you crash on the couch all night, I didn't hear the end of it for days."

She was too tired to argue. And too embarrassed by the memory of what he'd been doing to her moments before in her sleep to want to stick around and be civil.

"Don't be pissed at me," he said, pulling her to her feet before flopping into her recently vacated spot and grabbing the remote. "Can't blame me for wanting you to have a good night's sleep before hitting the highway in the morning. Oh, and I've got a few presents for Dillon and Fiona laid by the door. Tell your sister I expect to see them both at the pub for New Year's Eve."

"You're not going to have breakfast with me before I go? I'm not planning to leave until around eleven." She was almost to the narrow stairway.

"I won't be home. I have to work at the shop tomorrow and try to get those last-minute Christmas Eve sales."

3

"You work too much," she said, trying to hide the trace of genuine concern in her voice.

"It's not work when you love it," he said, flashing that devil-may-care smile of his at her. "One of these days you'll figure out what you want to be when you grow up and you'll understand."

There. Classic Toby. Equal parts cocky and dismissive. With a side of charm that made it all the worse. Problem was, if she picked a fight with him over this, he wouldn't have a clue what he'd said to insult her. Because to Toby, she was a kid. She might be twenty-four and aimlessly floating from one nearly completed degree to another, but that didn't mean she didn't know what she wanted to do with her life. She just needed to narrow it down. And that wasn't childish. It was smart. She was trying to be like Toby. Find the one thing she wanted to do with her life above all else and then rock that world to its core.

Making him take her seriously when she tried to tell him was too much work. After Christmas she was going to have to do something about this. The rent was awesome, but living with Toby was taking its toll. Hopefully there'd be enough early January dropouts to leave a housing vacancy. Having the most eligible bachelor in St. John's for a housemate wasn't all it was cracked up to be.

"Don't stay up too late," she said, stifling a sigh. "Night, Toby. Have a good Christmas."

She was three steps higher when he replied.

"Merry Christmas, Hannah." A pause. And then, even

though it was hard to hear, she knew he'd said it. "Wish you'd come out tonight."

Argh. This always happened with him. He'd say something, just some little thing that would set her into overanalysis. Did he care for her at all? Or was she misinterpreting? Again?

The wise thing to do at this point would be to go to bed. But she was a sucker for punishment.

Standing her ground on the stairs, she turned.

"Yeah?"

"Yeah," he said, leaning his head back against the sofa, the glow of the television flickering on his face. "It would have been nice to—"

His cell rang, that annoying classic phone ring that could wake the dead.

"What are ya at?" he said, answering the call with a deep voice that she knew was reserved for booty calls.

The indignity. She should just march up to bed. Right now. Instead of waiting for him to finish his call. Instead of breathlessly wondering who was on the other end, and if he'd leave the house in about five minutes.

She didn't want to listen. But when it came to Toby, she was helpless. Another reason to move out. How was a girl supposed to find a decent guy when her soul was in a constant state of flux?

"I have to work in the morning," he said to whomever it was. "Had to call it an early night."

Only Toby would call four o'clock an early night.

"Sorry, I can't." Pause. "No, really." A sigh. "I'm not giving you the brush-off. I've just been busy with work lately."

Go upstairs! Stop listening. Stop torturing yourself. Just go.

Following through on one's thoughts was harder than you'd think.

It was easier to walk back down the stairs, plop on the sofa next to him, and make faces.

"Oh please, Toby," Hannah whispered. "There's a chill in my bed only you can fill."

He gave her a stern look.

"Listen, drop down to the bar for New Year's Eve. It'll be a grand time, and I'll see you then," he said to the girl on the phone.

Hannah clasped a hand over her chest and sighed her best woe-is-me moan.

With a quick flick, Toby reached over and grabbed her foot, triggering an instant tickle. Trying to pull her foot away only made it worse as he jammed the phone under his chin and lunged for her other foot.

"Don't!" she screamed.

"I gotta go, darlin'," he said into the phone. "Take care."

And without even checking to see if the call had ended, he let the phone drop onto the blanket between them and proceeded to tickle her senseless.

"Stop," she panted. "Stop! Seriously. You'll make me . . ."

There was no way she would suffer the indignity of saying she'd wet her pants. But if he didn't stop, that was going to be the very likely outcome.

It took a bit more begging and pleading, but finally he stopped. Then he tousled her hair. That condescending little action of his always drove her off the deep end. Why couldn't he ever touch her like a man would touch a woman? It was always playful. Teasing. Like an older, annoying brother.

Hannah pulled herself to the far end of the red microfibre sofa, her hands creating a barrier.

"I thought you were going to bed," Toby said, lying back and unfurling his long legs on top of her.

"I figured you'd be out all night. After all, it's Tibb's Eve. I thought you'd be too drunk to see. How many nubile young lushes tried to coax you into being an early Christmas gift? Besides the one who just called?"

"Despite your opinion of me, I am not knocking boots with half the city. And it's been a long time since I've gotten drunk at work. It's bad for business. And me."

"My mistake. Just a quarter of it, then?"

He sighed. "Hannah. You wound me. I'll have you know that in the past six months I have gone home with exactly— Forget it. It's none of your business who I sleep with."

Hannah hated the hollow silence that filled the room. She wasn't equipped to keep quiet or still. But she didn't want to go down that road tonight. What she needed to do was go to bed. But come tomorrow it would be the beginning of a whole week or more without seeing him. An annoyed Toby was better than no Toby at all.

"Was it busy tonight?"

"Packed."

"What band did you have?"

"The Rummers."

"If it was that busy you could have called me. You know I'd love the extra cash."

His laugh erupted like a great deep geyser. "I told you, you had your first and last shift at the Banshee the night you dropped that tray of glasses."

Folding her arms across her chest, she looked into his eyes. "How many times do I have to tell you that was an accident? I was trying to unload the dishwasher. It's not my fault I slipped on a cherry."

"If you'd only stacked the glasses two high, it wouldn't have been an issue. You couldn't even see over the pile you had in front of you."

"Doesn't matter. It was the cherry. Cherries have no business in an Irish bar. I don't know what kind of place you're running. Seriously, if someone wants a drink with fruit in it, send them up the street to the fancy-pants gin bar. You shouldn't serve anything but rum, whiskey, and beer."

"Duly noted," he said, stretching out even more. "Wanna rub my feet? They're aching from running around delivering all those fancy drinks."

"Eww, get off me." She pushed his legs off hers and stood up.

"They hurt pretty bad. Come on, be a good friend and rub my feet. I'll have you know Tibb's Eve feet are in the top five aching category."

"You have a category for how sore your feet get?"

She was curious, but not enough to take off those socks and go to work on his size-eleven feet.

He laughed. "Not really. But I do have a category for expected busy nights. Number one, Paddy's Day weekend. Two, George Street Festival. Three, Asher Corbin drop-ins. Four, New Year's Eve. Five, Tibb's Eve. Really, I should just run Tibb's and New Year's together and call it Christmas week."

"But the bar's not open tomorrow, is it? Or Christmas Day?"

"No, even I close for those. But Boxing Day it's business as usual."

There was a stereotype about Newfoundlanders, that they loved to drink and party into the wee hours of the night. Even tonight, Tibb's Eve, was all about drinking. The night before Christmas Eve marked the end of the long, dry, fasting portion of Advent and was the most acceptable time for good Catholics to dip back into their spirits.

Toby's business relied on that stereotype. But there was a reason most of his regular customers were in their twenties. Even the most devout party animal had to settle down at some point. Hannah had been on that wild ride, but since both of her sisters had moved home to Newfoundland, she found herself thinking differently about herself, her future, and her role as the wild child of the Nolan family.

A lot had changed for her since Fiona, and then Grace, had returned. Not that Grace had really returned. She was home for a bit during the fall, but was now on tour with her boyfriend, rock and roll bad boy Asher Corbin. Hannah was still shocked that her geeky, quiet sister was with one of the world's most infamous celebrities.

She glanced at the clock. It was almost four thirty. Grace's flight got in a little before noon. Hannah wouldn't get six hours sleep before heading to the airport to collect her sister at this point, but it didn't matter. There was a big bed waiting for her at home, and she planned to curl up in it with her sister tomorrow afternoon and hear all about life on the road.

"I'm going to bed," she said. "You want me to open the curtains for you so the sun will wake you for work?"

"Thanks."

One whole wall of the living room was a large window, and as she pulled the curtains back, she was delighted to see soft, fluffy flakes of snow falling. The window overlooked St. John's harbour with all the boats lit for Christmas and the low sprawl of downtown in the background. This was the best view in the city.

"Did you get your snow tires yet?" Toby was more alert than he'd been previously.

"I . . . um. . . . No. I haven't gotten around to it yet."

"You knew you were going around the bay for the holidays, and you didn't get around to it?"

She let out an exasperated breath. "No. I had a little thing called final exams to worry about. And end-of-semester assignments. I'll get it done when I go home."

"You're going to drive in the snow tomorrow, Hannah."

And the night had been going so well.

"Good night, Toby. Have a great Christmas. Call me if

you feel the burning need to practise being the second coming of my father."

She stomped up the stairs and slammed her door. Just like she was sixteen. No wonder he treated her like a kid. If she was going to act like one, she bloody well deserved it. She flopped face first onto her bed and pulled her duvet completely over her body like a tent.

The last thing she heard before letting out a muffled scream into her pillow was Toby's deep voice bellowing from downstairs.

"Good night, Hannah. I'll miss you."

TWO
‿

To say Toby Sweeney was having a piss-poor morning would be putting it too kindly. The lack of sleep he could deal with. It was all the other crap life was throwing at him.

He'd meant to sleep until eight. That would give him two hours to get a shower, grab a bite to eat, walk to the music shop, and get things ready for the Christmas Eve rush. But he hadn't gotten up until quarter past nine. So, no breakfast.

He normally jogged to work in under ten minutes. But this morning he was forced to walk in the snow. When he'd left the house in the Outer Battery, the name for the houses tucked into the towering cliffs on the north side of the narrow harbour entrance, the snow was still light and fluffy. By the time he turned into the wind blowing a gale down Water Street, the snow was getting smaller and falling more heavily. It took more than twenty minutes to get to work.

Once he'd made it to the shop, he had to shovel the side-walk and a few of the metered parking spots in front of the storefront. By then it was past time to open, so there was no time to run to the coffee shop next door for a bite to eat and a cup of tea.

He'd just mopped up the wet, sloppy snow trail his boots made on the floor when he felt his pocket vibrate. He reached in, grabbed the phone, and was more than surprised to see it was Grace Nolan. Not that he'd never spoken to her before. He had briefly. But he was pretty certain she wasn't on his contact list, and there was no way he had that pretty face anywhere on his phone. A closer look, and he realized he had Hannah's phone.

The phone continued to vibrate, so he answered it.

"Hannah's phone. Toby speaking."

"Hi, Toby." Grace's voice was soft and cheerful. "Can I speak to my sister, please?"

Definitely the most polite of the three Nolan sisters.

"Wish you could, but I grabbed her phone by mistake this morning. I'm not at home."

"Oh no! Can you get a message to her? We're supposed to fly in this morning, but we've been delayed in Halifax because of the snow. We're not going to get in at all today. Do you think she'll check the arrivals information before she heads to the airport?"

That seemed much too prepared for Hannah. Even if she stopped to contemplate the snow coming down, there was a chance she wouldn't think flights would be cancelled. Hannah was used to the world bending to her will. Snow wouldn't dare impede her plans.

"Maybe," he said, noting the sound of hopefulness in his voice.

"Is there another number I can try to reach her at?"

"Sorry, Grace. There's no land line. You can try my cell and see if she answers." He gave her the number. "And you can email her."

"Thanks, Toby. Have a great Christmas."

"You too. Hope you get home for some part of it."

She laughed. "Ted is determined not to spend Christmas in Halifax, that much I know for sure. If we can't fly into St. John's, God only knows where I'll end up this Christmas."

Once they hung up, he cast a quick look out the window. The snow was picking up. There was little chance of any flights getting into the city with weather like this.

He dialled his cell, hoping Hannah would pick up. It went directly to voice mail. That was a good sign. She might be talking to her sister right now.

Still, he doubted that was the case.

The jingle of the bell over the door took his attention away from the plight of the Nolan girls. A snow-covered soul stamped his feet before he and Toby launched into a long discussion about which fiddle made a better gift for a ten-year-old girl.

The snowy dad was followed by the lady with the frost-nipped nose who made his day by purchasing eight albums of traditional accordion music, plus a couple of DVDs. And then there were the two girls who nearly collapsed on the floor once they made it inside the store.

"My God, you can't see a hand in front of your face out

there," one said, pulling off her red hat, spilling snow on the already sopping wet floor.

Her friend giggled. "Isn't this the best last-minute shopping trip ever?" She pulled her glasses off and blew on them, trying to combat the steam that had formed on them the instant she'd gone from cold to warm air.

"Can I help you ladies find something this morning?"

They looked around, as if just noticing where they were for the first time.

"Maybe," the one with glasses said. "Honestly, we needed to get out of the snow for a minute. We're trying to get to the craft shop up the road. It seemed like a fun idea to go shopping in the snow, but we didn't expect it to turn so stormy this quickly."

The girls flipped through the albums and music books aimlessly, stopping from time to time to marvel at the instruments on display. They were having a debate over whether a harmonica would make a good gift for Charlie when Hannah's phone rang again.

Of course it would be Fiona. Toby didn't think a day passed when Hannah didn't talk with her eldest sister.

He didn't get a chance to speak once he answered.

"Tobe, why do you have my sister's phone?"

"I knew you were talented, my darlin', but I didn't think clairvoyance was one of your skills."

"I was talking to Grace," she said. "But why do you have Hannah's phone?"

Her tone was somewhere between cross-examining lawyer, which she was, and overprotective sister, which she certainly was. Basically, it was the tone she used whenever she worried Toby had broken his promise to leave her baby sister unscathed.

"I grabbed it by mistake this morning."

"How?"

"Pardon?"

"How did you grab it by mistake?"

He liked Fiona, but sometimes she needed a reality check.

"Well, they were lying there side by side on the night table, and it was an easy mistake."

"Tobias Anthony Sweeney, you had best be joking."

"And if I'm not?"

There were sputters from the other end.

"Chill your boots. I'm kidding. I was running late this morning, and when I saw it on the coffee table, I thought it was mine."

"I don't see how that's possible. Hannah's phone has a very distinctive case."

"It had a distinctive case. Before she cracked it. Now it has no case. Just like mine."

She sighed. "I'm sorry. I know you wouldn't ever look at Hannah that way. Forgive me? You know how I get."

You know nothing at all.

This was Toby's plight. His daily struggle. Having to suppress the growing feelings he had for the baby of the Nolan family. All because of a promise he'd made to Dillon and Fiona when they'd agreed to let him and Hannah rent the house that there would be no funny business between them. It had seemed a stupid promise to make. Hannah was too young for him, and even if she wasn't, she damn near hated him. Plus, Dillon was his best friend. His business partner. The closest he had to a brother. They'd always had a standing oath that if one said not to even glance at a certain female, the other didn't. It was the way it worked. And while Toby had often made Dillon stay away from girls, his friend had never asked him to stay away from one before. Likely because Dillon had always been the ladies' man, the one all the girls wanted. One was as good as the other, as far as he was concerned. Until Fiona.

Oh, Toby had always done okay with the ladies. But he didn't have Dillon's level of charm, or Dillon's gifts of verbal seduction. It also didn't help that Toby wasn't a musician. If you could play a guitar, or sing a song, then there were plenty of women ready to fall at your feet.

Toby had to work for the women he got. Although since Dillon had gone off the market, his allure seemed to have gone up. It was fun for about a month. Now it was a nuisance. Mainly because the one girl he wanted was off-limits. Off-limits and yet always within reach. It simply wasn't fair.

"Have you been in touch with Hannah? She's not driving home in this weather, is she?" Toby said.

"We haven't heard anything from her yet. When are you closing the shop and heading home?"

"I was planning on staying open until four or five."

"Even if the city shuts down?"

"As long as the buses keep running, I'll stay open. Listen,

I gotta go. Despite the weather, I've got customers. Have Dillon call me later."

"Toby, Hannah needs her phone. We need to talk to her, and she's not answering yours."

"I'll send it home in a cab."

It was another ten minutes before he could call for a cab. As he expected, they were backed up. People had to get around on Christmas Eve, and it was easier to let a cabbie do the driving.

A cab finally pulled up in front of the shop a little past noon.

"Can you drop this off to the red house out at the end of the Outer Battery?" Toby said, leaning into the open window and handing the phone to the cabbie.

"Buddy, you're cracked. I don't drive out that road on a clear day, let alone with the roads like this." The cab driver cackled at him, the smell of stale smoke wafting out. "The plows haven't even touched all the main roads yet. It'll be days before they get to the Battery."

"Can't you try?"

"I wouldn't even try to get up the base of Signal Hill on a day like this."

Through the limited visibility of the snow, Toby couldn't see anyone fighting their way up the street.

"Calling it a day?" Mr. Burton said, locking the doors to his watch shop next door. "No point staying open. It's not fit out for man nor beast. Have yourself a Merry Christmas."

Toby raked his fingers through his snow-drenched hair.

"Can you wait just a couple of minutes?" he asked the cabbie.

"I'm going to start running the meter."

"Of course you are."

He turned and shook the elderly watchmaker's hand before dashing inside the shop.

Grabbing the money from the till, he stuffed it in his bag. He'd worry about totalling the cash later. A quick check to make sure the temperature was set right so the instruments wouldn't warp, and then he armed the security system. With a sigh, he flipped the sign hanging on the door from open to closed, shut off the lights, and jumped into the waiting cab.

The radio was cranked up, but instead of Christmas tunes, there was a running commentary on the weather and road conditions.

"You're my last fare," the cabbie said. "They're pulling the buses off the roads."

In St. John's, there was no more sure a sign of impending stormy weather than the bus company shutting down. Once that happened, doctors' offices, government offices, and the university all followed suit. Within an hour, the city would be at a standstill.

"Is the mall closed?" Toby couldn't help but ask. He often wondered if business would be better if they were located in the mall.

"Won't be long now, and they'll have to. Christmas Eve or not, you can't fight Mother Nature."

It took the cab as long to drive to the base of the hill as it had taken Toby to walk the same route just a couple of hours before.

"This is where I stop driving. Twenty bucks, if you please."

Thrusting the cash into the driver's hand, Toby didn't have the spirit to wish him any Christmas greeting.

It was going to be a cold walk back to the house.

THREE
ॐ

Hannah's morning started out great. She'd woken a little after nine, not at all tired. It was Christmas Eve. She was going to spend Christmas with both of her sisters for the first time in four years. And it looked like it was going to be a white Christmas. There was no better place to celebrate than in Heart's Ease.

While in the shower, she planned out the day. After she picked up Grace, they'd get home by maybe two if the roads weren't too bad. She'd have to take her time, but they'd get there in one piece. Poppy would likely have a big feed of fish and brewis cooking, and there'd be a crowd gathered for some music. They'd sing and dance and eat until it was time for Midnight Mass. If it was still snowing, everyone would bundle up in snowsuits and walk to the church. By one thirty they'd be home to open their presents.

This time tomorrow she'd be slowly waking to the smell of turkey roasting and salt beef and puddings boiling on the stove. It was going to the best Christmas of her adult life. She had a feeling deep in her heart that this Christmas would create an indelible experience.

It wasn't until she went downstairs that she realized there was a major storm brewing. Living in a house that overlooked the harbour, you learned to tell how foggy it was by the limitations of what you could see. This was her first winter in this house, but she imagined it was tenfold for snow.

There wasn't a hope of seeing any part of downtown. The towers of the Basilica were impossible to spot. Even worse, she could barely see the rigging of any of the crab boats directly across the harbour. The lighthouse at Fort Amherst was a ghost.

With a sinking heart, she went to grab her laptop and check the flight status. She clicked and double-clicked, and still the wi-fi wouldn't connect. Another casualty of the weather. Maybe she'd have better luck with her phone.

After twenty minutes of frantic searching, she hadn't found her phone. But she'd found Toby's. It was lodged in the crease of the cushions on the sofa, as dead as a doornail.

With an aggravated scream, she went to the kitchen and boiled the kettle. A cup of tea would calm her down and help her think what to do next.

One thing was certain. It was pointless to even go to the airport. There was no way a plane could land in this weather. She should load the car and get on the road. It was still early enough that she could take her time and get home.

Bundling up in her yellow parka, she wrapped a long scarf around her neck and pulled the hood tight, tying it with a sturdy knot under her chin to keep it from blowing down. She stomped into her boots, grabbed the presents Toby had left by the door, and headed out to her battered Civic.

The wind nearly knocked her over, and it took every bit of balance she had to stay upright and get to the car. The wrapping on the gifts was quickly blanketed by snow as Hannah dropped them into the trunk and closed it with a firm smack.

The narrow lane that passed as a road to the houses along the Battery was untouched. There wasn't a tire track in sight. The snow shouldn't be hard to get through. It wasn't built up yet. Being a stone's throw from the ocean had its perks.

Back and forth four more times, and she had the car loaded. Out of desperation she searched once more for her phone, but the bloody thing was lost. Her final act before leaving the house was to run up to Toby's room. His bed wasn't made, which was unusual for him. He was pretty meticulous about keeping things tidy. She pulled the grey and green quilt into some semblance of order and then laid his gift on the bed. There. If he came home today, he'd see it.

He'd been vague about his Christmas plans. He was always vague about anything to do with his family. Still, whenever he made it back to his room, he'd get it. She briefly wondered if he'd be alone, then shut down that train of thought. No point making herself miserable.

In under five minutes she was sitting in her car, waiting for the windows to defog. She listened intently to the latest road report, a sinking feeling in her stomach as she heard about the whiteout conditions on the highway. The police were warning people to stay off the roads.

At this point she had two choices. Stay put or take her chances by adding a couple of hours onto her drive by sticking to all the coastal roads through the towns and harbours that wound along the shore of Conception Bay and Trinity Bay. She needed to call home. If she risked a drive like this without talking to her parents, she'd never hear the end of it.

Shutting off the car, she walked to the O'Tooles'. Their squat little forest-green house had withstood a hundred and twenty years of wind, rain, and snow. She banged on the wooden storm door that was firmly latched. The O'Tooles weren't too old. They were in their early seventies, but Mrs. O'Toole was hard of hearing and Mr. O'Toole was about three hundred pounds, and his every step was laboured and measured. Between them, it usually took a good three or four minutes to open the door. She wasn't waiting it out.

"Hello?" she yelled from the small porch. "Hello? It's Hannah, from next door. Can I come in?"

A thump. The first telltale sign that Mr. O'Toole was on his way. "Yes, my lover, come on in," he called, his old-school townie accent thick and rich.

"I was wondering if I could use your phone?"

"Who's that?" a shrill voice called from down the hall.

"It's the young girl from over the way," the man bellowed.

"What?"

"The young girl from over the way. You knows, the one who takes you to bingo."

Hannah had driven Mrs. O'Toole to bingo once, about two months ago.

"Oh, the sweet young one."

Hannah smiled.

"No, the other one. The one who likes to talk." He gave her a smile and dropped his voice. "You're better than sweet. I've always liked a sassy girl."

It didn't make her feel any better.

"Put on the kettle," Mrs. O'Toole yelled. "We'll have some tea now the once."

"Oh, no. Thank you, but I can't stay. I need to make a quick call and then get on the road."

"On the road? In this? No, my treasure, you won't be driving this day. You can make your call, but that's about all you'll be doing."

She hoped not. She was counting on the weather being better in Trinity Bay.

"Do you have long-distance?" The phone was an old rotary-dial monster mounted to the wall in the kitchen.

"Yes, all our kids are on the mainland. You could call Timbuktu and it wouldn't cost us extra." The man eased himself into a tattered recliner in the corner of the room.

Well, there went any notion of privacy.

Her mother answered on the fourth ring.

"Mom," Hannah said, her voice starting to shake. "I don't know if I'm going to get home."

"Oh, praise Jesus," her mother said, a loud sigh of relief evident in her voice. "You're not on the road. We've been trying to reach you."

"I can't find my phone."

"Toby has it."

"What? How do you know?"

"Your sisters have spoken to him. But never mind that. You are not to budge from the house until this storm passes. Your father is on the way to an accident here in the harbour. The roads are like a sheet of glass."

"It's that bad out there?"

"And getting worse. The wind is fierce. What's it like in town?"

"Not that windy," she said, despite feeling the wooden house shudder. "Well, maybe it's picking up now."

"Dad said to tell you that as soon as the weather breaks, he'll come in for you in the rig."

The rig is what they called their monstrosity of a four-wheel drive.

"Don't be foolish. If it clears, I'll come out."

"You certainly won't."

"Mom, I've never missed a Christmas at home."

"It happens to all of us at some point. It's never easy. But hopefully by tomorrow you'll be on your way. We won't open any presents tonight if you're not here. Or Grace. We'll postpone Christmas until we're all together."

Tears threatened to seep from her eyes. The last thing she could do was make her mother worry further.

"Thanks, Mom. I'm sure it'll blow over quick."

Then the lights blinked. Once. Twice. Hannah held her breath. But the power stayed on.

"Mom, the lights are flickering. I'm going to go back to

the house and blast the heat in case we lose power."

"Call us when you get your phone back."

"I will, promise." She didn't have the heart to tell her mother that she might be alone. God only knew when Toby would come home. He certainly wouldn't be back until after dark, once he shut the store down. And even then, he might have plans.

"Don't worry, my love. We'll see you as soon as we can. Just stay inside and be safe."

"Merry Christmas, Mom." Her voice was almost a whisper.

"It'll be Christmas when you're in the harbour, and not a minute sooner," her mother said. God, that woman always knew how to put her in a better mood.

Since she wasn't going anywhere, she stayed for a quick cup of tea with the O'Tooles before bundling up again.

"Now, if you're still home tomorrow, we're having dinner at noon. You come on over. There'll be plenty here. We've got a roast of moose."

Despite thanking them, she couldn't help think that the last thing she wanted for Christmas dinner was moose. Moose wasn't a Christmas dinner. Nothing but a plump, juicy turkey would do. Fingers crossed she'd get her wish.

FOUR
ॐ

Walking into the wind in a raging snowstorm, Toby made a list of all the things he was going to do when he got home. First he was going to defrost himself in the hottest shower he could manage. Then he was going to toss an entire package of hot wings in the oven, crack open a case of beer, and spend the day watching almost three months' worth of recordings of *Hockey Night in Canada*. Working Saturday nights meant missing out on one of his favourite TV experiences.

It was his Christmas Eve tradition. He ate frozen food, drank too much beer, and watched hockey. No one knew this, of course. Even Dillon was under the impression that Toby went to his grandfather's for the holidays. His private business was his own, and he didn't care to share the Sweeney baggage with anyone.

The only hitch in his plan was Hannah. He wasn't sure how she was going to feel about his plan, but he didn't care.

She could suck it up and watch hockey, or go watch her own TV in her room.

A small part of him, a wee fraction of his soul, perhaps, was glad she'd be around for at least a bit of Christmas. For starters, he wouldn't have to keep her presents hidden much longer. And if he was willing to let himself really dwell on it, it would be nice to have someone around to say Merry Christmas to on the actual day. In person. In the morning, like normal people did.

But that all depended on the weather. There was a good chance the clouds would blow offshore in a few hours, and he had no doubt that when that happened, a parade of loving family would swoop in to rescue her and bring her safely home.

Must be nice.

He looked up and spotted the red clapboard of the house. Even in the snow you couldn't miss it. He was equally relieved to see Hannah's car still there. He had faith that even a woman as rash and headstrong as she was wouldn't risk her life to get home for the holidays. But it was reassuring to know that he was right.

He reached out to open the door when the knob slipped from his hand as the door was yanked from the inside.

"You're home!" Her exclamation sounded cheerful. "I'm so glad. Oh my God. You walked in this? You must be freezing."

She yanked him into the porch and whipped his hat off his head.

"You're like a snowman. Don't track all that wet snow onto the floor."

Hannah never ceased to amaze him with her power to jump from idea to idea, without ever stopping to wait for responses. Sometimes watching her around the house made him tired. But he also found her compelling, captivating like a spark sizzling in the air, flitting around trying to decide where to land. And when it did, everything became brighter and slightly more dangerous.

"Are you hungry? I'm cooking."

"You are? I didn't know you could cook."

"I can cook. I just don't like to. And it's not that hard. It's only following directions. It's basic chemistry, when you think about it. And I'm great at chemistry."

He sniffed the air. There was a comforting, if unidentifiable scent coming from the kitchen.

"Smells edible."

"Thanks for the vote of confidence. Just wait till you try it."

"Is it ready, or can I shower first?"

"It can hold. Are you freezing?"

"I was. But there's a wave of heat coming from in there." He nodded toward the door that separated the porch from the rest of the house.

"Yea, I've had the heat on bust. I'm afraid we're going to lose the power."

"We're not going to lose power. But we might run out of furnace oil."

Her face dropped. "Do you think?" Then she ran back into the main part of the house. He suspected she was turning down all the heaters.

Pulling off his boots, he went into the main portion of the house and stopped mid-step.

"You've been busy."

That was an understatement. The floor was covered in strings of coloured lights, and a sickly green artificial tree stood in the corner of the living room. He thought it might have been the tree and the decorations that were in the pub when he and Dillon had bought it from Glen Molloy ten years ago.

"The Internet is down. I'm afraid the house is going to blow into the ocean. And I thought I'd be alone all day. I had to do something to make it festive here. Do you hate it?"

Earlier in the month he'd come home to find Hannah decorating for Christmas. There'd been a slight blow-up about how early it was and how he hated people overdoing the holidays. She'd finally capitulated and taken down the few decorations she'd put up. He'd felt terrible after the fact, but he was one of those bah-humbug guys at heart. He pretended he was ambivalent about it, but deep down Toby hated holidays. He decorated the bar because he had to. But he could draw the line at home.

A few times since she'd hinted at decorating, but he'd managed to convince her it was pointless since she wouldn't even be around for the main event.

"I don't hate it." Liar. "It's very . . ." He cast a look around the room. "It's very vintage Christmas."

"I know. I found most of this down in the basement. I don't know where Dillon got this stuff." She reached down into a box and pulled out a long length of multicoloured foil.

31

"Do they even make this tacky shiny garland anymore? Still, it's fun, and it's better than nothing, right?"

He couldn't say no. It would hurt her feelings. And if he had to share the house with her for the next day, when he knew how much she'd wanted to be with her family, well, he'd suck it up and pretend he gave a damn about this stupid holiday.

The smile he pasted on his face was surprisingly only eighty per cent fake. Her delight in decorating was disturbingly contagious.

"Absolutely. I'm going to grab a shower, and then we'll eat whatever it is you've magically created from our sparse groceries. After that, I'll help you tackle those lights."

God. Was it really going to be Christmas lights? Long before his parents had done the wise thing and divorced, Christmas always began heading downhill the instant his father started in on how his mother put the lights on the tree. Well never mind. John Sweeney was on the wrong side of the sod to pass comment on Toby's or anyone's lack of tree-lighting skills. And his mother . . . well, who knew where she was hanging her Christmas lights these days.

As he stripped off and stepped into the steaming shower, he pushed all thoughts of his family, or lack of, aside. It wouldn't do to get maudlin now with Hannah here. Until she could get home to her own family, he'd have to step up and make sure her ruined holiday didn't get any worse.

∂

Hannah had just finished wiping down the counter when Toby came back downstairs. The hairs on her neck tingled. It was ridiculous how giddy she felt around him. With the storm raging, it was unlikely he was going anywhere today. She'd be spending one of her favourite holidays with the man who had her stomach in knots and her heart in a spiral.

On top of it all, she was cooking for him. What had started as a simple cooking experiment to help her feel better about being stuck in town was now a chance to show that she wasn't as hopeless around the house as he thought. If she'd known she would be showing off her cooking chops, she would have tried something a bit more exotic than quiche. Although she was hard-pressed to think what else she could have made. Aside from staple breakfast foods, neither of them tended to eat at home. At least it wasn't bologna and eggs.

Please, God, let this be edible!

"This looks really good," he said, sitting down at the small table she'd set.

"Thanks," she said. "Tea?"

"Absolutely."

It was one thing they had in common. They both adored tea. Not fancy tea. Just plain old orange pekoe. Tetley. Red Rose. King Cole. Neither of them cared. So long as it was liberally laced with sugar and Carnation canned milk. It was a Newfoundland staple. Most kids grew up on the concoction but advanced to more mature tastes with age. It was Hannah's comfort food. And Toby had told her once something similar, in one of the rare moments she got him to talk about anything other than the here and now.

There were secrets to Toby that made Hannah wonder who he was underneath the good-time-guy exterior. He was great at deflecting questions without you noticing it. It drove her mad, since she was pretty much an open book. Aside from her yin-yang feelings for him, there wasn't anything she didn't share with him. Or anyone else for that matter.

"Oh, I have your phone," he said, laying it on the table. "You might want to call home."

"I did. I went to the O'Tooles'. The second everyone knows I have my phone back, there'll be nothing but calls. It can wait till we eat."

She caught the look he gave her.

"What?"

"I just thought you were glued to your phone, and your sisters."

She shrugged. "I'm hungry."

"Then let's eat. I've walked in this storm twice today, and I didn't get breakfast. I might let you have one piece. A small one."

While she'd poured the tea, he'd served up two big slices of quiche.

"Have you made this before?"

"A couple of times with Mom at home. It was in the recipe book she'd made for me when I first moved to town. She started it with Fiona. Simple recipes that she figured we could manage on our own with a student's budget."

"It smells fantastic. What's in it?"

"A bit of this, a bit of that. Whatever I could find that I thought might taste okay."

She noticed that he didn't take a tentative small bite to test the waters. He dug in, shoving a huge piece in his mouth.

"Mmmm," he said. Followed by something else she wasn't sure of. And then another *mmm* as he loaded his fork again.

Something fluttered inside of her. A good something. Warm and exciting. He'd made this sound of happiness because of her.

"Bacon," he said. "And cheese. And something spicy. It's perfect."

"Chew your food," she said, laughing as he cut off another slice and heaped it onto his plate.

There was very little dinner conversation, other than Toby's musings on ingredients and banter, once it became clear he really was going to eat the entire thing.

"These freeze well, don't they? I seem to recall people making quiche and keeping them in the freezer for when they need them."

She shrugged. "I have no idea."

"Then that's it. I want one of these in the freezer at all times. Seriously. I think you've just become the best roommate I've ever had."

"Even better than the one you lived with for two weeks and all you did was have sex?"

Crap. She wasn't supposed to say that. Wasn't supposed to know it.

"Dillon told you that, did he?"

He didn't seem embarrassed.

"Fiona. But I guess he told her."

"Well, Marianne was a roomie with perks for sure. But she was stalker material. That's one of the many great things about living with you. You tolerate me at best. There's no need to worry about you falling in love with me. It's perfect."

Dear floor. Open up and swallow me now.

"I didn't mean it in a bad way," Toby said. "I know I annoy you. I don't do it on purpose. Hell, half the time I don't even know how I provoke you." He extended his hands in a helpless gesture. "Maybe it's because you don't have brothers."

"Do you have brothers?"

He never spoke of his family. She'd just assumed he was an only child who wasn't close to his parents.

A flash of steel crossed his face.

"No. Just a guess based on watching Dillon's interaction with his brothers."

"Are you seeing your grandfather tomorrow? Having dinner with him?"

"No. He's. . . . Hey. How about we get started on those lights?"

"Don't want to talk about it?"

"Nothing to talk about." The smile he gave her was pure fool's gold. He stood and started clearing the table.

"Okay. But, Tobe, you know, you don't annoy me that much. Most of the time. And if you ever need someone to talk to about, well, anything, I can be a pretty good listener. Really. I do know how to shut up from time to time."

"I'm good." He hesitated. "But thanks for the offer. I'll do the dishes and be right out. You should call home."

How had she never noticed it before? The firm set of his face, as if he were holding something inside, using all his physical strength not to let it out. Too often she'd seen this look and mistaken it for disregard. Understanding dawned on her. This look wasn't directed at her. It was all internal. There was a battle raging inside that man, and she was going to make it her goal to make sure he came out on the winning side.

FIVE

Three hours, seven beers, and two packs of silver tinsel carefully placed and recklessly removed from the branches. That's what it took to finally get the tree looking festive. Hannah was impressed with their work. Toby hadn't grumbled at all when she'd pointed out bare spots with the lights. Nor had he protested when she had him straighten the star on the top of the tree three times.

"I think we're done," she said, hands on hips, eyes squinted so she could see empty holes.

"There's no thinking to it. That's as good as this old tree is going to get. And I think as a reward for my hard work, I can now rest in peace and watch hockey." Toby grabbed his beer and fell onto the sofa, remote in hand.

"Hockey? On Christmas Eve? No way!"

It wasn't supposed to come out in a shriek, but she couldn't help it.

He levelled a calm glare on her. "And why not?"

"Because. It's not. . . . It's too. . . . Well, you can watch hockey any time. This is a holiday. You don't do normal things on a holiday."

He laid down the remote.

"If you were home now, what would you be doing at four p.m. on Christmas Eve?"

"I wouldn't be watching hockey."

"Evidently. But what would you be doing?"

"I'm not sure. Mom is making a pot of baked beans to bring up to Poppy's tonight for anyone who doesn't want fish and brewis. Chances are I wouldn't be helping with that. And if Dad isn't working, he's likely checking in on some of the older people, bringing them cards and making sure they're not too lonely. Sometimes I go with him. But it's most likely I'd be wherever Fiona is."

"And if she were with Dillon, and he was watching hockey?"

"We'd be telling him to turn off the TV because hockey is not a Christmas Eve activity." She laughed and poked his shoulder. Teasing was the only way she could ever touch him. "Thought you'd wrangled me into defeat based on a technicality, didn't you? Gotta work harder than that. I have a lawyer for a sister. I see a trap coming from a mile away."

"Okay, you've got me. No hockey. For now. So what is an acceptable activity?"

The smile he gave shook her to her toes. This easy-to-please version of Toby was confounding.

"Since we can't go outside, we could watch a movie."

"What are the conditions?"

She tried to think what kind of loophole he might create to justify slipping a hockey movie into the mix.

"It needs to be Christmas-themed. Holidays, trees, family." That should do it.

"Something set on Christmas Eve even?" He'd already picked up the remote and was searching through all the on-demand films.

"That would be perfect! I'll go get the popcorn. You want beer or something else?"

"Beer is a long-standing part of my Christmas Eve tradition."

She couldn't argue. It was a part of hers as well. While she pulled together their movie feast, he called out from the living room.

"Just so we're clear, I'm giving up my game, so as long as the movie I find falls into those categories, I get to choose, right? And you don't get to try and change my mind."

Quick checklist in her mind: holiday, family, Christmas trees, Christmas Eve. Perfect.

"Absolutely. You're the Christmas flick boss."

"You're going to love this. Best Christmas movie of all time, hands down."

Once the popcorn was popped, the cold beers were opened, and she'd snuggled down on her end of the sofa, a soft grey throw wrapped around her legs, he pressed play.

"What are we watching?"

"You'll know it when you see it. It's a classic." He reached into the bowl of popcorn and grabbed a handful.

"Bruce Willis? I don't think I've seen this. I think the only Bruce Willis movie I have seen was that one about the ghosts."

Bruce and some guy were on a plane chatting about air travel. He was a cop. And then the title of the movie came crashing in, the two words sliding in from opposite sides of the screen.

"Hell no! *Die Hard* is not a Christmas movie."

She reached for the remote.

Toby pressed pause before holding it out of her reach.

"It is a Christmas movie."

"Come on, Toby. This is an action flick. One of those shoot-'em-up gangster movies."

"*Die Hard* is not a gangster movie."

"Well, whatever. I'm sure it's got guns and fighting in it, so it's not Christmas."

"You're sure it's got fighting?" He laughed. "Have you seen this movie?"

"Of course not."

"Of course not?"

"Why would I? It's old, it's one of those mediocre eighties action movies that are totally unbelievable."

"It's a classic. And it is full of Christmas themes like family togetherness and coming home for the holidays and all that jazz. Didn't you hear the flight attendant say Merry Christmas? Hear the sleigh bells? I can't believe you've never seen this movie."

"I grew up with two sisters. Do you really think our movie choices included shoot-'em-up action movies?"

"You've been denied a vital part of growing up. That's it. You have to watch it now."

She lunged for the remote, landing on his lap.

"No. We're not watching it." Her hand flailed around, trying to grab the long black device, which he managed to keep out of reach. Damn long arms.

"You want this?" He shook it around over her head. Then, with the speed of a ninja, he dropped it down the neck of his shirt.

Hannah froze. If she wanted it, she'd either have to reach up under the shirt or undo the buttons. She also became acutely aware that she sat facing him, her legs on either side of his, their chests mere inches apart. As were their faces.

"Too timid to go get it?" There was a challenge in his voice, low and subtle. His eyes were brighter than she recalled.

"No."

God, why did she have to sound so uncertain? So breathless?

Something shifted in the room. The careful dynamic of their house-sharing, the unspoken law of no flirting, no overt touching, it seemed to be blown away with the storm galing outside.

The subtle arch of his brow was a question mark, a hazardous dare to test the waters.

"If you want to change the movie, you'll have to force me. If not, kindly sit back and trust me that you will enjoy this."

Her mind was in shambles. Was he talking about the movie? Or something else? Was she reading too much into something so simple? It didn't feel simple.

Tentatively, she reached toward his shirt. Halted. She was a fool. There was nothing here but her overactive imagination. She wanted more. Wanted to believe that this was a challenge, not about watching a movie, but about something deeper, more tangible. And if she acted on that, she was going to make a fool of herself.

Rolling off his legs, she quickly shifted back to her safe corner of the sofa.

"I'll give it fifteen minutes."

It was hard to be sure, but a small part of her thought he might have sighed. Toby leaned over and rubbed her hair.

"Atta girl. Give it thirty. And if you're not hooked, you can choose the next one."

"I don't like these kinds of movies. I don't have a big stomach for violence."

He wiggled his way down the sofa a little until their elbows touched. "It's not that bad. Just give it a try. And if it's too much, you can always hide under the blanket."

Or bury her face in his protective arm? Oh, he didn't say it. Maybe he didn't even think it. But Hannah was choosing the subtext of this conversation, and that was the new unspoken agreement, as far as she was concerned.

Blame it on the beer. Or the way Hannah looked all damn afternoon. Christ, she was doing her best impression of a sultry red-headed Christmas angel in a whisper-thin white sweater that pulled tight in all the right places. He'd been aching all afternoon to tug at the little bit that threatened to fall off her right shoulder. It didn't even matter that she was wearing the most ridiculous leggings, with little white reindeer and snowflakes. At one point in the afternoon, when she'd stretched to place a bulb high up on the tree, he'd gotten a little jealous of the deer that got to spend all day cozied up by her tight little ass.

What was this game he was playing? Hell, why didn't he just drop the remote down his pants and beg her to go for it? That was it. No more beer. It was clouding his common sense. It was one of the reasons he'd gone for this movie. He hadn't watched a lot of holiday movies, but he had a feeling they were all dripping with sentimentality and love, and he didn't need either of them feeling lonely and yearning for more.

Not that it was likely Hannah felt anything for him. Although for one endless moment, as she'd straddled him, he'd thought she might have felt a smidgen of the desire that threatened to burst through his tightly woven dam of resistance. But it had passed as quickly as it had come. For her, at least.

Neither of them had spoken since around twenty minutes into the movie, when Hannah had announced that while it wasn't a Christmas movie, there was no point in stopping now that she was invested in the film.

He was glad she was enjoying it, because all he was able to focus on was the way a long piece of her wavy, dark red hair curled slightly inward toward her breast. If that wasn't distraction enough, there was also the alluring scent of spice that subtly caressed him from time to time.

It was a new scent for her. He couldn't keep track of all the perfume bottles he'd noticed lining her dresser. Not that he'd been in her room for more than a minute or so at a time, usually when he was looking for a sweater. It used to annoy him how she'd grab any sweater of his that he left in sight and wear it without asking. Now he liked the excuse to tease her, and there was the added benefit of it smelling like her afterward.

"Are all action movies this insanely good?"

Like a startled kid, he jumped at the sound of her voice. "What?"

"I'm conceding defeat. This is a great movie. And since I've never seen an action movie before, I'm wondering what else I'm missing out on."

"I guess I know how we'll be spending most of the winter. We can work our way through Willis and then graduate to some modern stuff."

She wrapped her long, elegant fingers around her beer bottle and took a large drink.

"Does that mean you're going to stop working every Friday and Saturday night?"

"I'm thinking maybe I can trust Billy to supervise one of those nights. Perhaps. I'll see how it goes over the holidays."

"You need to start delegating more. You can't run two businesses and expect to work most of the heavy shifts yourself." She paused the movie. "Pee break. You want another beer while I'm up?"

"It's not even eight. I think I need a break. I'm starting to feel it."

"It's food we need," she said as she tossed the blanket at him. "What's in the freezer we can pop in the oven?"

The freezer. He'd forgotten the load of wings and potato skins he had planned to gorge on today.

"I've got just the thing. Leave it to me." He extended his hands, and she pulled him up. "God, this is the laziest day I've had in eons."

"What would you have been doing today if we weren't snowed in?"

The standard lie started to form, but he couldn't do it. Not with her, not when she was still holding both his hands, the coloured lights of the tree casting dancing shadows on her face.

"This, basically. More hockey. More beer. But less fun."

"You weren't going out with friends, or going to see your grandfather?"

He shrugged. In for a penny, in for a pound.

"Well, I would have worked until at least four or five. And then I might have dropped in somewhere on the way home. But by now I'd be right here, doing this. Now wipe that sad look off your face. I like this. I like getting some time for myself."

"But you can't be alone for Christmas."

"It's not like I lock myself in the house. I see people over the holidays. It's this day. It's my day of rest."

"But why?"

He dropped her hands and walked to the kitchen. Hannah followed at his heels.

"It's just my way." He shrugged, as if casting off her question. "Now I'm going to toss some food in the oven. You go do your thing, and we'll get back to seeing if Bruce lives to die hard another time."

"Why do you never talk about yourself?"

The faucet was his saviour. Turning it on made it easier to avoid her questions, and he wouldn't have to pretend he hadn't heard.

Too bad she was like a cat stalking a shrew. She turned off the water.

"Nice try."

Reaching into the freezer, he grabbed the wings. "Since your need to use the bathroom isn't that strong, grab me the baking sheet, will ya?"

Feather soft at first, then warmer and more a caress, her hand on his shoulder froze him to the spot.

"I'm not going to beg you to share anything with me. I get it. You're the strong silent type. But if you ever want to let that wall down, I'm—" She stammered. Took a breath. "I'm your friend. You can talk to me."

All thoughts seemed lodged somewhere between the brain and the tongue. He didn't move, didn't speak. Didn't want the heat of her touch to leave his skin. Maybe if he stopped breathing he could preserve this feeling, this spark of longing.

The fire inside escalated when she slid her other hand over his back.

"I mean, that's what we are, right?" The soft rasp of her voice tore into his heart. "We're more than just roommates. We're at least friends, aren't we?"

Choices. He was always trying to make the right ones.

The right choices for the business. The right choices to help his friends. The right choices for his grandfather. But when was the last time he'd made the right choice for himself? For what he needed? He didn't need another friend. He needed the promise of Hannah's touch. He needed the hope that she felt even a fraction of the desire he did.

Slowly he turned toward her, caressing her face. Screw Dillon and Fiona and their rules. It was time to think about what he needed for a change and let the rest of it fall where it may.

"I don't know what we are. But, yeah, we're more than roommates. One thing is for damn sure." He rubbed a thumb across her lower lip, feeling the tremor that coursed through her. "I've waited too long to do this."

SIX

~

Hannah felt like she was under water. Everything was moving slower than usual, and there was an invisible pressure pressing her forward, toward the man she'd longed to touch for so long. Toward the man who was gazing at her as if he'd just caught Santa laying out presents under the tree.

When their lips connected, it wasn't a frantic kiss. It was slow. Testing the waters, worried it might be too cold, terrified it might be too hot. Hannah had dreamed of this kiss, dreamed of it and tried to blot it from her groggy morning memories.

Sweet baby Jesus, there was nothing in her dreams that prepared her for the reality of kissing Toby Sweeney. There was a small niggling part of her brain that briefly wondered if the impetus for this kiss was his avoidance of sharing anything about himself, but there was something in the way he'd looked at her, in the way he'd spoken to her, that convinced her, this wasn't an escape from sharing.

It was the opposite. This was his way of sharing. She felt

it in the way he tangled his fingers in her hair, in the way his lips tasted her, as if taking small, gentle bites of a soft fruit, and more than anything, in the way he let a small groan escape when she returned the kiss in kind.

She wrapped her arms around him, pulling him closer, aching to feel him against her. A small part of her recoiled at how cliché she felt, at the way her legs weakened, the heat that ensconced her body, the roaring in her ears. It was the kind of reaction to a kiss that romance movies made their money from. The kind of kiss women knew was impossible to find in real life.

A shudder rocked the house as the wind outside tried to batter its way into the house. He gripped her tighter, his kiss becoming more demanding. The windows rattled as the snow beat relentlessly against them. As if daring the elements to try to stop what this was between them, Toby pushed her against the kitchen window, its chill on her back adding to the frantic push and pull of the elements of desire that were rapidly taking over her body.

Then with a loud crack, the house went dark.

That was enough to pull them apart.

"Are you okay?"

Toby pulled his lips away but kept a firm hold on the rest of her body.

"I'm okay. More than okay." Her laugh was shaky. "But I hope this is just a power bump."

"I think a transformer blew."

He slid a hand into hers and led her carefully to the living room. The house was eerily silent other than the hammering of the wind and snow. Not a spark of light could be seen.

"It's hard to tell if it's a local outage or not because there's nothing to see beyond the snow."

"I don't really care," she said, pulling him down onto the sofa beside her. "We don't need lights or heat to continue."

Nothing mattered right now other than feeling him. Being with him in the ways she'd dreamed of only the night before.

Her eyes were slowly getting used to the dark, and she was certain she saw him smile. She shivered when he stroked her hair. "So you're not sorry?" He kissed her brow. "Not going to write it off as a mistake? A momentary lapse in judgment?"

"Are you?" She had to whisper it because she was afraid of the answer.

"I don't do anything I regret. If I kiss you, you can be damn sure I mean to. And I want to again."

Storm be damned. Blackout, smachout. The only thing that mattered was quenching this thirst for him.

It was hard to tell who kissed who first, but it was hot and intense.

This is a kiss that leads to sex.

There was no denying the thought. It was going to happen. And it would be mind-blowing.

If only her phone would stop ringing.

"Ignore it," Toby said, slipping a hand under her sweater.

"I am." She slipped a finger into the waistband of his pants.

The ringing stopped around the same time he cupped her

breast. His fingers teased her nipple through the thin lace of her bra.

It started ringing again, almost right away.

She tore her lips away from him, feeling the empty chill in the air.

"I'll turn it off."

"Just answer it. I know your phone. Whoever it is, they'll keep calling till you answer."

"It's my mother."

With a groan, Toby rolled off her. "Don't be long. I'll be right back. I can't sit next to you and not touch you."

From deep inside she felt a heat that she'd never experienced before. He wanted her. He wanted her so badly that he couldn't trust himself around her. Her cheeks hurt from the wide grin that took over her face.

"Hi, Mom," she said, willing her voice to sound normal.

"Honey, how are you?" Gail Nolan sounded frantic.

"I'm great." Wait. She shouldn't be great. She should be pining for a Christmas with her family. "Well, all things considering. We have no power. I think a transformer blew. But it's still pretty warm here. Hopefully it'll be back before long."

"Not according to the radio. I suppose you don't have a battery-operated radio to listen to, do you?"

"I have a phone, Mom. I can go to a website. Or Twitter. I don't need VOCM to keep me in the know."

"Well, you haven't bothered yet. If you did, you'd know that most of the province is in a blackout. This storm is hitting hard, and a couple of main generating stations are down.

So are some powerlines. Newfoundland Power is warning it might be twenty-four hours until power is restored to everyone. And that's if the weather improves."

"It's fine, Mom. Toby will figure it out. I'll stay safe and sound in the house."

"But what about food? And water? And heat? As soon as the sun is up tomorrow morning, storm or no storm, Dad is coming to get you."

"Don't be foolish. You don't want him on the road if it's dangerous. We're all safe, Mom. We'll let Mother Nature have her way and work it all out after."

"But I thought you wanted to come home for Christmas?"

"Of course I want to be home. But not if it means risking life and limb to do it. We've got plenty of food to tide us over."

"But how will you cook it?"

"Mom. You know we don't cook much. When I say food, I mean chips and bars, cereal, cheese and crackers. Just make sure there's a big turkey waiting for me when I finally do make it home."

"Oh, Hannah. This is terrible. Why did you have to wait so long before coming home? If you'd come yesterday or the day before, everything would be fine. You'd be here with us."

"Mom, I had to finish my assignment. And I had to work. You know I—"

"We've got a big fire going in the stove, and we're all walking up to Poppy's now for a feed. The skidoos are going crazy here bringing people out for a visit." Clearly her mom was in full rant mode and didn't really care what Hannah had to say.

"It's just like Christmas was years ago, before electricity. But I can't enjoy it because I miss you. And Grace. Poor Grace."

"Poor Grace? Isn't she on her way to some Caribbean island right now? Must be nice to have so much money that if Asher can't get her home for Christmas, he can just whisk her off to a tropical paradise."

"I don't like that man."

That was an understatement. Hannah's mother still hadn't forgiven Asher for seducing her daughter, the good girl of the family, the smart one, the sensible one, and taking her on the road with him. It didn't help that she hadn't met him yet. They'd only been gone a month or so, but Hannah's mother was certain that she'd never see Grace again. It was better to change the topic, because if you encouraged her to talk about it, she'd be on the phone for hours.

"What's the latest forecast saying?"

"There's no end to the snow in sight. But if the wind would calm down, we'd just have a heavy snowfall instead of this blizzard. The snow is supposed to let up by Boxing Day."

An hour ago, this news would have had Hannah in tears thinking about missing Christmas. But now, all she could think of was keeping warm with Toby for days on end. And there was only one way to keep warm. The fun way.

"It'll be fine, Mom. I'll see you all soon."

"Don't you worry, we won't have Christmas without you. No one is touching a present until you are home and in your Christmas nightie. Wait until you see this year's fabric!"

Ugh. The Christmas nightie. Every year their mom made

all of them matching flannel nightgowns to wear. They were comfy. But her mother wasn't the best seamstress in the world. There was a reason Hannah never uploaded any Christmas morning pictures to her social media accounts.

Still, it was another family tradition, and Hannah knew the time would come when she'd miss those things. At least this year her mom was waiting for her. Unlike her sisters, Hannah had gotten to wear her nightgown with her family for every Christmas of her life.

"I'll see you as soon as I can get home. Love you, Mom. Have a fun night."

"Be a good girl, Hannah. And tell Toby we wish him a Merry Christmas."

"I will."

"And, honey, if you think he's going to be by himself, you be sure to bring that boy home with you. He could use a good family Christmas."

As she hung up, Hannah was relieved to know that she wasn't the only one who thought Toby needed some holiday TLC.

SEVEN

Toby tried not to listen in on her conversation with her mother, but he couldn't miss the sadness in Hannah's voice when she said she wanted to be home. What did that feel like? Wanting to be with your parents? Having them miss you right back? He decided there and then that as soon as the storm broke, he was taking Hannah to Heart's Ease. But before he could do that, he had to make sure they didn't freeze to death.

The lights were only out about ten minutes, and already the drafts from the wind were ripping through the house. It wouldn't take too long for the place to significantly cool down.

"We need candles," he said. "Do you have many?"

Hannah laughed. "Are you kidding? Candles are the gift that keeps on giving. I must have a dozen or so."

"Go get them. Do you have a flashlight app on your phone?"

"I do! I never thought I'd need it, but goes to show what I know."

Before long she was back with an armful of candles. "There's more, but these are the biggest ones. I figure we shouldn't burn them all at once." She started setting them around the living room.

"Perfect. Light them up, and then I need your help."

While she'd collected candles, he'd gone for blankets.

"Four enough?"

The soft golden glow was perfect. And it made her look even more seductive, however in the hell that was possible.

"Great. Now come give me a hand."

He held one edge of a blanket and gave her the other. The staple gun made sure the blanket attached firmly to the wall, creating a barrier between the kitchen and the living room.

"What are we doing?"

"We're going to try and keep all the heat in this room, and keep out the drafts from the windows and doors. With no heat, it's going to get cold soon."

"Oh, I can think of ways we can keep this place heated." She trailed a long finger down his arm. His cock leapt at the touch.

"I like the way you think. But it's not making the heat I'm worried about. It's keeping it."

It took two blankets to cover the big picture window, but in under ten minutes they had a nice cocoon made.

He was tempted to move the two of them to his room, but that seemed a bit too presumptive of him. Two kisses wasn't an invitation to make love for hours on end. Shit. He didn't mean that. Making love. He wasn't going to make love to

Hannah. He didn't do that. He had sex. Great, no-expectations sex. Love had nothing to do with it.

Of course he cared for Hannah. He liked her. He worried about her. She was his friend. Maybe more than a friend. But as far as emotions went, this had nothing to do with love. It was all about chemistry. She was majoring in chemistry. She could understand that.

"What are you thinking?"

Her breath was warm on his ear.

"I was thinking about chemistry. About warming up with you."

Her laugh hit him in the heart. Another warning sign that he might be in over his head.

"I'm getting cold already," she said, bounding to the sofa and covering up with one of the three quilts he'd brought down.

"Do you want an extra sweater?"

"Ask me again in an hour."

God, her voice had dropped to a husky tone that lodged in his groin. If there was no sex tonight, it was going to be pure hell on earth being this close to her and not getting to play out the fantasies he'd tried to keep at bay for so long.

On the other hand, why rush it? He'd waited this long. Drawing it out could be just as erotic.

"We have a long night ahead of us," he said, settling in next to her, extending his arm and feeling her snuggle in beside him. She fit perfectly. "I was thinking we could talk a bit."

She toyed with his fingers that were draped over her shoulder.

"Really? Just talk?"

"Not just talk. But, yeah, I want to talk as well. We talk a lot, I know. But it's normally playful. Or argumentative. And there are some things I'd like you to know."

"About you?"

"You don't have to sound so incredulous."

"I'm sorry. I'm just used to you shutting me down or changing the topic any time our conversations have turned to you. I'd love to talk."

"It's about you as well, you know. About what just happened. What I hope will happen. For starters, I haven't slept with anyone in a while."

"How long is a while?"

"I can't say, exactly. It's not like I marked it down someplace. But it's been a while. Ever since I realized—"

"What?"

Deep breath. "Realized those other women were a poor substitute for you."

She scooted out from under his arm and perched herself on his legs so she was facing him. One thing he'd come to expect from Hannah was an absence of coyness. She didn't disappoint.

"So you've thought about me as a—" She twirled her hair and looked away. He knew she was trying to find the right words. "You've wanted me?"

"Wanted you? I've wanted you for as long as you've been

coming to the Banshee. But you were young. And a flirt. I'd find myself looking around the bar on a Friday night, wondering what was missing, and only realizing it was you once you'd slip through the crowd to order a drink. Never the same thing, mind you. Do you know how frustrating it is for a bartender not to be able to anticipate a regular customer's order? I was just working up the nerve to do something about it when you showed up with Fiona. And you know what happened then."

"Do I ever. Everything was about her and Dillon. Man, that was a summer of drama, wasn't it? But enough of them ruining a good thing." She gave him a feather-light kiss on the lips. "What I don't understand is, if you've liked me for this long, why you haven't done anything about it since we moved in. Wait! Did you move in here because I was moving in?"

"No. I had the house first. It was only after I swore on my father's grave about a million times to Dillon and your sister that I would not, under any circumstances, have anything other than a strictly platonic living arrangement with you, that Fiona offered the place to you."

"Fiona did what? I'm going to kill her. It's okay for her to fall in love with the devil of Heart's Ease, but I can't—"

"They didn't know. They didn't know that I was interested in you." He wrapped a strand of her dark red hair around his finger, his other hand languidly touching her leg, her back, her arm. "Maybe if I'd told them, maybe it would have been different. But as far as they're concerned, I'm not ready for anything other than one-night stands. I can't blame her. And until I knew that I wanted more from you than just one night, I wasn't going to do anything either."

"Did you know? How I felt, I mean? Did you know I've had . . . not a crush. That's too childish. I'm not sure how to describe it. But you're all I've thought of for as long as I can remember. Even when I was dating Eli, I kept going to the Banshee in the hopes that you might say something." Her fingers tangled in his hair as she spoke.

"Hell no. If I'd known, well, who knows. I thought you hated me. I was preparing for you to move out."

"I was thinking about it. The bickering started just so I wouldn't go crazy wanting you. It made it easier, but you're so bloody good at it that I came to hate it." She kissed him again, that soft, gentle kiss that set his heart and everything else on fire. "And now here we are. Snowed in. In the dark. Nothing to do but talk and—"

This time her kiss wasn't soft and quick. It was firmer, more insistent. Her way of saying *less talking*.

He pulled his lips from her and trailed them down her neck, talking as he went.

"There's more I want to tell you."

"There's more I want to ask. And tell you. But you said it first. We have all night. We can do both. And right now, if you stop touching me, I'm going to move out."

"I'm not going to stop." He kissed her mouth again. Then back to her neck. "But you best prepare yourself, because I am not having sex with you tonight. I've waited this long to feel your body, learn how to make you squirm, that I'm not rushing it now."

"I can make you change your mind."

"I expect you'll try. And I expect it'll be hard."

Jesus. She reached down and stroked him through his jeans. "No expecting required. You are."

"Try your best, you evil woman, but we are going to start this relationship right. No rushing into anything. I plan to have you begging me to go the distance. And I might concede in a couple of weeks."

"Weeks? You're not serious."

"You can attempt to convince me to change my mind. I can't guarantee it will work. However, you're welcome to try your best."

He wasn't sure where this had come from, but now that he had her in his arms, so close, he realized that this might be the most important thing he ever did in his life. Something in his gut told him that he needed to go slowly. His happiness depended on it.

EIGHT
∾

Hannah woke up alone and cold, despite a pound of blankets on top of her. There was a faint glow coming through the blue fleece blankets that covered the window. Despite her best efforts, she was still wearing all of her clothing, but her lips were aching from the marathon of kissing that had happened overnight.

There was one thing she could safely say about Toby. The man could kiss. And he had a willpower that needed serious scientific study.

At one point in the night she'd begged him for more. His response had made her heart ache, and that might have been the point when it dawned on her that she had to be careful with Toby. She had the power to hurt him in a way he might not recover from.

She'd been fumbling with his zipper.

"Goddamn it, Tobe. I'm not a kid. You don't need to take it slow for me. I want you. Now."

He'd pulled her hands up and planted a kiss on her palm.

"I want you, too. But I've learned that anything worth having, worth keeping, is worth waiting for. I'm not saying this to hurt you, so please don't take it that way, but I'm sick of women wanting to rip my clothes off, come, and then go. I want more with you. I want to take you out, want to make out with you, and go to bed aching for more. More than anything, I want to give you time to get to know me. Know all the stupid things from my past that might make you want to run away. I'm not rushing this, because I want you for more than a night. More than a week. And you need to know things that I can't just blurt out all at once during one romantic snowbound night. I have baggage that no one knows about. I'm not heaping it on you after the fact."

"Is it why you hate Christmas? Why you had no plans for the holidays?"

He'd stopped. "You're pretty perceptive, aren't you?"

"People always underestimate me. I have a scientific brain. I'm going to be a doctor. I'm not dumb."

"You're going to be a doctor? I thought you were going to do your master's or go into pharmacy?"

"I've been on the fence. I hadn't told anyone yet. I'd planned on telling Dad first. For Christmas. The third-generation Dr. Nolan. Now you know. Merry Christmas! I'm applying to med school."

"If my father weren't already dead, he'd die of disbelief if I told him my girlfriend is a doctor. Or will be."

There was a lot in that sentence. It was hard to choose what to focus on. Depth trumped vanity.

"Your dad was a jerk, wasn't he?"

"Pretty much."

"Your family is a mess?"

"That's putting it mildly."

It was clear that while he wanted to tell her things, he wasn't in the mood at the moment.

"I'm not going to push. You can tell me when you're ready."

He'd kissed her then. A kiss that spoke to her soul. A kiss that was both thankful and promising.

They'd fallen asleep shortly after that, every part of her toasty warm except for her head.

Now she was cold and alone. Dear God, had her dreams about Toby turned so lifelike that she couldn't tell reality from fantasy?

"Ho, ho, ho."

"Toby?"

He peeped out from behind the tree.

"I was hoping you wouldn't wake up yet."

"What are you doing?"

"Putting your presents under the tree."

"Presents? You got me more than one gift?"

She'd laid his gift there yesterday when they'd decorated the tree. She hadn't said anything when he hadn't added to it. At that point she was still under the illusion that he merely tolerated her.

He smiled. "I don't have a lot of people I buy gifts for. You. Dillon. Fiona. My staff. That's it. Ready for your first gift?"

"Let me get up and go to the tree." She started to sit.

"No. Hold on a second. Stay there for this one."

Standing, he reached to unhook the blanket from the window. It was still snowing, but it was a light snow, fluffy and beautiful. From where she sat she could see the harbour stretched out before her, the city snow-covered and beautiful in the distance.

"I know it's not the harbour in Heart's Ease, but this looks pretty awesome, doesn't it?"

"It's beautiful. If I'd ever planned on being away from home for Christmas, I think I would have been a mess. Somehow, you've made this a perfect Christmas."

"I'm glad you think so. It's already the best Christmas I've had in about twenty-five years."

Math was one of her strong suits, not that it took much to do the math on this one. He hadn't had a good Christmas since he was six. She planned on fixing that.

The hardwood floor was freezing. She pulled a cushion from the sofa and sat on it next to the tree.

"I only have one gift for you. You should open it first."

He shook his head. "No. You first."

The first box reminded her of home.

"You sure this is from you? I always get a gift about this size every Christmas Eve from Mom. If there's a flannel granny-gown in here, I'm not going to be impressed."

"First of all, if there's anyone who could make a long flannel gown sexy, it's you. Second, when I shopped for you, I didn't think we were anywhere near me being able to purchase fancy nighties. No worries, though. I plan to fix that as soon as the mall opens."

"Keep talking like that and the only thing getting unwrapped on this floor is you."

"Open it, you temptress."

As she pulled back the layers of tissue paper, she found a green two-toned hoodie, very similar to the blue one he owned. The one she borrowed the most.

"Are you trying to give me a hint?"

He laughed. "Maybe I was getting tired of looking for mine. But I did pay attention to details. I know you like this style the best, and I ordered it in my size, because I have a feeling you like them baggy, since you never wear any of your own."

She tossed it to him. "Wear it for a day or so and then give it back to me."

"What?"

"I don't wear your sweaters because I like them better than mine. I wear them because they smell like you."

"Are you serious?"

"Like a heart attack. I love the gift, and I'll love it more when it's been Sweenied."

"Sweenied?"

"Yeah, infused by you."

Shaking his head, he handed her another present. "I'll figure you out at some point, I suppose."

"Never."

The second box contained a stethoscope.

"What is this?" Her voice went up in surprise.

"It's not a good one. I just wanted to help you figure things out. Which I guess I didn't need to do, since you made up your own mind. Hey. Why are you crying? I'm sorry!"

"No, don't be." She wiped her eyes. "It's just that you were thinking about me. This is a really thoughtful gift, Toby. Like, amazingly thoughtful. Not thinking about me in a general way, but thinking about me as a serious person, thinking about helping me get my bearings."

"Then why are you crying?"

"Because I'm just starting to realize that yesterday, last night, everything you said was true. You do like me."

"Like you?" He was next to her in an instant. "I more than like you. It's complicated for me, since I'm not good with emotions, but I know that you're special. Unlike anyone else I've known. Am likely to know."

"You know that if you'd given me this gift I'd have known, right? I'd have clued-in to how you feel."

"I don't think that's true."

"It's true. There's symbolism in this gift, Toby. You might not see it, but I do. You could have said nothing, and this gift would have told me everything."

She couldn't let this moment pass.

"Kiss me."

"Yes, ma'am."

Holding up a finger, she stopped him. "That's what I

would have said the instant I opened this gift. Wouldn't have mattered when it was, who was here, or where we were. This gift gives you instant rights for kissing."

"That would have surprised me."

"You've surprised me."

His third gift was simpler. It was a photo of her car. On the back of it, he'd written a note: *Snow tires. Installed. It's a good thing you have me. Merry Christmas.*

"You can't buy me snow tires."

"Too late. I have. And they're on your car. You've been driving on them for a week. You're not as perceptive as you thought."

"Why would you do that?"

"Because I didn't want you dying on me. And you seemed in no rush to get it done. I didn't want you going home for Christmas on banana peels."

"Toby, this is too much. Tires are expensive!"

"You can make it up to me."

"You want me to pay you back?"

"Don't be foolish. You can show me your gratitude in that kiss you asked for and then denied me."

She popped a quick peck on his cheek. "Not until you open your gift. I'm embarrassed now. It's not nearly as thoughtful as your gifts. But I hope you like it."

Holding her breath, she waited.

"Tickets to a hockey game. Movie money. And a gift certificate for dinner at—no way, Hannah. That's too much. That place costs a fortune."

"You bought me tires and you're going to question how much I paid?"

"Fair enough. But this is. . . . This is a date. Several dates. You gave me three dates for Christmas. What would you have done if I hadn't invited you?"

The words were hard to say, but they were true. "It would have told me it was time to move out. I needed to know. And you do like all of those things, so it was only half-selfish. I mean, you'd enjoy it all even if I didn't go with you."

It was sinking in just how stupid her gift was. It wasn't thoughtful at all. It was manipulative.

"Toby, I'm sorry. This is a terrible gift. I'm taking it all back. I mean, we can go if you want. But I'm going to spend all year finding the perfect gift for you. I swear."

He pulled her into his arms. "Hannah, stop. It's perfect. You know I don't like stuff. I'm always complaining about clutter. Experiences are always better for me. This is a great gift. And just so you know, this is sort of my version of the stethoscope. You gave me dates. Trust me, I would have known who to ask."

"Really?"

"Absolutely. Now, can we have that kiss? We have a busy morning ahead of us."

"Sleeping? Kissing? Maybe third base?" She nuzzled his neck, the idea of keeping warm on the sofa becoming ever so appealing.

"Not today, my Christmas angel. We're going to shovel, and hope to God a snowplow has hit the road. Either way, we're putting those tires to good use and getting you to Heart's Ease. You're having Christmas with your family if it's the last thing I do."

NINE

It took nearly twice as long as usual to get there, but a little after two they pulled up next to the Nolan house. He'd been to Heart's Ease before, but there was something magical about the place today. The snow was still glistening white, and there was a tranquil peace in the tiny village. A few times Hannah had asked him to stop the car so she could lean out the window and wish someone Merry Christmas.

One elderly woman had handed them a fruitcake. She was walking with a cane and picking her way gingerly through the snow. "I was going to walk down to give this to your father, but I can't handle the chill today."

"Aunt Ida, get in the car. If you slip I'll never hear the end of it."

"I'm fine to walk. The house is just back there. No need to go out of your way."

Hannah was out of the car in an instant. "It will take us ten seconds to back up and get you home. It'll take you ten minutes."

"Mind your manners, I'm not that slow." Still, the woman relented and let Hannah help her into the front seat. Sure enough, her house wasn't far away. Toby walked her to the door.

"Oh, Gail will like you. You'll do fine. She's coming around on Dillon. She thinks Ted is the Antichrist. So you're already ahead of the others. Merry Christmas, young man. I have to say, if there were this many fine-looking young men around the harbour when I was younger, I might not have stayed single." She patted his cheek and closed the door.

"Did I just meet the infamous Aunt Ida Walsh?" he said as he got back into the car.

"You sure did. I think she likes you."

"I think she likes a lot of people."

"Only the good ones."

Toby shut off the engine and took a deep breath.

"You're staying, right? You're not just dropping me off and going home?"

"I'll stay for a while. But I don't know about staying the night."

She reached over and cradled his face. "If you go, I go." Her voice was gentle. "We'll do as much or as little as you want, but you are not going back to an empty house."

"Don't be foolish. You'd planned on spending the week here. And I can't stay that long. I have to work tomorrow night. You'd be home alone if you went back with me."

"You can get Billy to work if you want to. But no pressure. Think about spending the night. I bet Mom already has a bed made for you. Or if you're afraid of Dillon and my sister, you can go stay at his parents' house."

Her teasing created a steadfastness in him.

"I am not afraid of Dillon. And I'm not going to hide the fact that I care for you." Was that growling sound coming from him? "I'll stay for tonight at least. But no funny business. No sneaking into my room and having your mother add me to her list of men not good enough for her daughters."

Hannah laughed. "I'll try my best. Although as the baby of the family, I'm used to getting my own way, and getting away with it."

"Don't I know it."

Taking another deep breath, he opened the car door. Time to face the Christmas.

The scent of turkey and Jiggs' dinner met him even before they opened the door to the green saltbox house. His stomach grumbled. The last real meal they'd had was yesterday's quiche.

"Is the power back?"

"No. They have a gas stove. When the power goes here, the only problem is frozen pipes. There's enough kerosene lamps to light a village, and the wood stove is going all year round, anyway."

Hannah had just laid her hand on the door latch when the sound of barking erupted. There was a stampede in the house of setters and parents clamouring for Hannah's attention. Toby felt like an outsider, looking in on someone else's picture-perfect life.

He'd be better off sitting in the home with his grandfather. The old man might not know him anymore, but he'd be in familiar waters.

"Toby." Hannah's father, Dan, extended his hand. Toby shook it. "Thanks for getting our girl home." The tall man clapped Toby on the back and drew him into the kitchen. "Come on in. Leave your boots on. Gail has been sending me out to the shed all morning. It'll be good to have a young man around to do her bidding for a while."

"Merry Christmas, Toby," Hannah's mother said. Then he was pulled into a tight hug before a firm kiss was planted on his cheek. "I told Hannah last night to make sure you came home with her. I can't bear to think of anyone being cold and alone during the holidays."

He was practically pushed onto a kitchen chair.

"You two must be starving. Normally I'd make you wait till dinner is ready, but we're running late." The woman didn't stop chattering, yet she still managed to cut thick slices of bread, pour up piping hot tea, and dish out baked beans that were miraculously warm.

"These are wonderful," he said between mouthfuls.

"Hannah has the recipe. She only needs some incentive to cook it. Maybe this will do it."

"She's a great cook," he said. Her mother didn't need to know that he'd only made that discovery yesterday. "Her quiche is the best I've ever had."

Gail and Dan went quiet, and there was no mistaking the look they shared. Or the smile that crossed Mrs. Nolan's face.

"Of course it is. She learned from the best," Dr. Nolan said, pulling his wife into an embrace and kissing her cheek.

So this was family when your father wasn't a deadbeat drunk and your mother wasn't angry at the world for saddling her with a child when she was sixteen. He'd known families could be good. Hell, he'd seen it plenty. But there was something dangerously comforting about this one. Maybe it was the way they were dragging him into it, treating him not as a guest but as one of their own. Or perhaps it was a deeper knowledge. Something that told him that if things went well with Hannah, and oh how he hoped they did, that this family could actually be his.

"Dan, can you come upstairs and help me for a second?"

There was a look in the woman's eyes that Toby recognized. It was very similar to the way Hannah gazed at him just before they kissed. They were almost out of the kitchen before her mother stopped. Turning, she cast a glance at both of them.

"It's about time you two figured it out. All that bickering was starting to become monotonous." Her smile was wide as she left the room.

The second her parents disappeared, Hannah jumped up and wrapped her arms around him. It felt good. Better than good. Natural. Welcoming.

"I'm glad we figured it out as well. All these months not getting to do this."

She kissed him, wrapping her arms around his neck.

"You know," he said, pulling her onto his lap. "Before we lived together, all I knew about you was that you were sexy as hell. And it drove me wild. But the more I learn about you, the more it turns me on."

"Sexy as hell?" Her laugh was cute.

"Even in your lab coat with your goggles on."

"They're not goggles, they're safety glasses. And when did you see me like that?"

"Oh, how easy you forget. Remember the time I brought you supper when you had to work late? Or the time you forgot to grab your assignment off the printer and called begging me to fetch it for you?"

"You've been there for me this whole time," she whispered. "I was too blind to see it."

"You weren't blind. You were distracted. How could you see I cared, when I worked so hard to act like I didn't?"

"I'm not distracted anymore."

Toby couldn't stop looking at her. This beautiful woman who was giving herself to him. Then it dawned on him. From her rich, dark red hair that framed her perfectly heart-shaped face, to the way her deep green eyes glistened, Hannah was Christmas. It wasn't just the colours. It was the feeling of home that she gave to him. The way she made him feel warm and at ease. And more importantly, the way she gave him everything he'd ever wanted, just by being herself.

"Thank you," he whispered, burying his head in her neck.

"For what?"

"For giving me the best Christmas gift I've ever received."

Even her laugh was Christmas, like the soft tinkling of a bell.

"My gift sucked."

"Your gift was perfect. You've given me hope. You've given me a home. You've given me you."

Her voice was soft, like the snow that drifted down over the harbour. "Merry Christmas, Toby."

"Merry Christmas, Hannah."

I love you.

Whoa. Where had that come from? Too soon, buddy. Too soon. Luckily for him, there tended to be a three-second delay between the words in his mind forming and actually coming to life in his mouth.

He held on to Hannah, unwilling to let her out of his arms until the urge to say something ridiculous passed.

Surely it would pass.

TEN

~

Hannah peeked out the window, watching Toby shovel a path to her grandfather's house. The dogs danced around him, kicking up a mini-blizzard in the weather. About twenty minutes after they arrived, the snow picked up. Now it was coming down in droves.

"It's not that miserable out that he'll disappear." Her mother was elbow deep in water, rinsing her fine china. Even if they were "roughing it" without power, there was no excuse not to break out the silverware and good dishes.

Hannah's stomach fluttered. "I'm keeping an eye out for Fiona."

She wasn't going to fight with her sister on Christmas Day. But that didn't mean she wasn't going to let it be known how Fiona had no business telling Toby to keep away.

"Ow," she muttered, as the match in her hand sizzled closer to her fingers. The perils of lighting candles while gazing at the object of her desire were greater than she'd thought.

"I told her we'd be eating at five. Honestly, this having to eat two big meals in one day thing drives me off my head. She'll be so full now from Mona O'Dea's dinner that she'll do nothing but push around her potatoes with us."

"Mom, be nice."

"I am nice."

"I think it's good that we did supper instead of dinner. Dillon would have been with his family, and Fiona with us. This way, they get to eat together with both families."

Her mother sniffed. "I suppose you're right. And it's better than not having her here at all. Have you heard from Grace?"

Danger. Danger. There was no coming back from a Grace discussion right now. And she wasn't going to rub it into her mother's face that Grace was likely bikini-clad, sprawled on a beach in Tahiti, with Asher Corbin rubbing sunscreen all over her body.

"There's a couple of skidoos coming down the road. Maybe it's Fiona and Dillon."

Laying down the candle and matches, Hannah headed to the porch to see who was hiding beneath the face-masking helmets. Sure enough, under a red helmet emerged the beaming face of her sister, Fiona.

The dogs quickly abandoned Toby and pounced on the eldest Nolan. It was hard for Hannah to believe that Fiona, the sister who essentially ran away from Heart's Ease and never looked back, was now a member of the community. And that Sailor and Captain had bestowed their loyalty onto her.

Hannah loved Fiona and was happier than anyone that her

sister was home. But of all the girls, it was Hannah who had lived in the harbour the longest. She was truly the one who felt Heart's Ease was home.

Well, give it seven or eight years and she'd be back in town, working alongside her father so that she'd be the third Nolan to be the family doctor of Heart's Ease.

She'd love to have this house as her own, but it wasn't likely her parents would move. Still, she had a backup plan. There was a nice little piece of land behind the house. It was covered in stunted, spindly trees, but it wouldn't be that hard to clear out enough space for a small house. Her grandfather had told her she was welcome to it so long as she didn't build some garish modern monster. That wasn't a problem. She was totally obsessed with tiny houses, although since hers would be stationary, she could have six or seven hundred square feet to work with.

But that was putting the cart before the horse. First she had to get into med school. There'd be time enough for legacy planning once it was official.

Watching as Dillon and Toby hugged, her heart lurched. Toby. How strong was her future with him? Would he be willing to relocate to Heart's Ease if she practised there? Would he relocate anywhere?

There was no point thinking about that now. Sabotaging whatever was between them based on a far-distant future was counterproductive.

"Smells some good, Mudder," Fiona said, stomping snow off her boots as she stepped into the porch.

Hannah stifled a laugh. Fiona was a townie who'd adapted to the mainland quickly. Her forced attempts at Newfoundland dialect always sounded ridiculous.

"Merry Christmas, sis," Hannah said, wrapping her older sister in a tight embrace.

"Glad you made it out," Fiona said. "That was nice of Toby."

"Speaking of which, we need to talk."

Hannah pulled away and grabbed her sister's hand.

"Upstairs. Now."

"Let me get undressed first," Fiona said, unzipping her one-piece Helly Hansen skidoo suit. The blue material was faded, and Hannah suspected it had belonged to her father.

"Honey, finish lighting the candles. It's getting too dark to see."

"Any more fire in here, Mom, and we're going to spontaneously combust," Fiona said. Hannah had to agree. But at least she could use that as an excuse to drag her sister upstairs.

"There's a stack of pillar candles up in my closet. Come help me."

"No, you go get the candles," her mother said, donning a pair of oven mitts. "Fiona, run up to your grandfather's and get a couple of his kerosene lanterns. I'll need those here in the kitchen if I'm going to take up this dinner."

Fiona shrugged and pulled her suit back on. "Whatever it is, tell me later."

Hating that she huffed as she left the room, Hannah stomped up the stairs. If she was going to act like a petulant little sister, she might as well get it all out of her system while no one was around to tease her.

کو

"So, finally got you to Heart's Ease for Christmas," Dillon said, leaning against the white slab fence that separated Hannah's parents' house from her grandfather's.

"Couldn't let Hannah drive in this."

Toby tossed another load of snow out of the path. His back was aching. The snow was wet and heavy. But he'd be damned if Hannah's grandfather or his wife, Sadie, would slip and fall on his watch. Plus, it kept him out of the house. There wasn't a surface of the Nolan house that wasn't plastered in Christmas kitsch.

"I always knew you were a good Samaritan at heart."

"At heart? I'll have you know I've been doing good deeds for damsels in distress since 1998."

"Ninety-eight? That's pretty specific."

"That's as specific as I'm going to get for you."

Dillon picked up a wad of snow and pressed it into a tight ball. "Makes me wonder what other secrets you're not going to get specific on."

Despite the cold, wet snow that plastered his face, Toby felt his face go hot. If there was going to be a reckoning before the day was out, it was time to fess up. Just not now.

"Do you seriously want to challenge me to a snowball

fight?" Toby said. "Need I remind you of last Paddy's Day weekend and the Great George Street Snow War? I'm sure I still have the trophy at the bar."

"You only beat me because you got me plastered on rum beforehand. If this March is as snowy as last year, you can bet I'll be the victor."

There were things Toby knew well. His best friend he knew best of all. With an agile duck, he easily avoided Dillon's snow-packed missile.

"You asked for this." Without warning, Toby walloped Dillon with a shovelful of Mother Nature's best work.

And because he knew Dillon so well, the next thing he did was hop the fence and hightail it into the Nolans' porch, locking the door behind him for good measure.

"Running from Fiona?" Hannah's mother laughed.

"Nah, simple survival of the fittest." He refused to acknowledge that his relationship with Hannah was going to be an issue. He certainly wasn't going to admit it to her mother.

Dillon stood outside the door, arms folded, with a vivid array of murderous intentions dancing across his face. The last thing he'd do was bring snow into this house. He was still trying to convince Mrs. Nolan that he wasn't the Antichrist. Toby had the upper hand in this battle already.

Wiping her hands on her apron, she came to the porch and looked outside.

"Oh, I see," she said, walking to the door and unlocking it. "I'll tell you what I told my girls their whole lives." She opened the door and nodded at Dillon. "Don't start a fight you're not willing to finish." Then she stood aside as a snow-ball smacked Toby in the face.

With a whoop of delight, Dillon came into the house and hugged Gail Nolan. "That's the best Christmas gift I could have asked for."

She patted him on the cheek. "Don't let it go to your head."

"You like me," Dillon said, hanging up his coat.

"I like you," she replied. "Not as much as I like Toby, but you're growing on me."

With that, Toby laughed. A real laugh. One that came from a place of a long-vanished memory of family happiness. Instead of dissecting the memory, he chose to focus on the moment and let the laughter flow.

ELEVEN

∿

Boiled potatoes piled three deep. Cabbage, turnip greens, and brussels sprouts draining in faded orange colanders. Bright pink salt beef and riblets taking up almost as much room as the carved turkey. And more puddings than Toby had ever seen served during one meal: pease pudding, blueberry pudding, molasses raisin pudding, onion pudding, and bread pudding. The amount of food laid out on the counter was sinful. And he suspected the Nolans would be feasting on leftovers for the rest of the week.

"The table might be set for fine dining," Hannah told him, pushing a plate into his hands, "but we don't stand on ceremony. Fill your plate and make sure you come back for seconds. Mom will think you don't like it if you only consume about two thousand calories of food."

"She's right. I've been eating three plates lately just to make up for the insulting way I only devoured half a chicken the first time I was invited to dinner." Dillon's plate was piled so high Toby wondered how the gravy Dillon was ladling on could even penetrate the mound of food.

"I heard that," Mrs. Nolan called from the dining room. "And I'll let you away with one today, since you ate a couple of hours ago."

"It's a trick," Fiona whispered. "She'll be watching to see how much we eat, and then complain to me tomorrow about how your mother's dinner ruined our supper."

"That's the truth," Hannah said, the soft orange glow from the kerosene lamp placed on the window sill casting a mesmerizing glimmer in her eyes. "She'll be watching. Trust me. She dropped enough hints about it before you came."

The girls started giggling, and Toby felt that clutching sensation in his heart again. It was more than this new freedom to explore his feelings for Hannah. It was being part of something bigger than himself.

"You don't need to tell me to eat," he said, adding a third potato to his plate. "I'm famished."

Hannah laid a hand on his arm. He didn't miss the look that passed from Fiona to Dillon. Turning away from his friends, he focused on Hannah, who he suspected made that gesture to get her sister's attention.

"Think carefully before you answer this question." Her other hand hovered over one of the serving platters. "Beef or ribs?"

"Neither."

"What?" There was an echo in triplicate.

"I don't like any of it. Never have. It's too salty."

"Too salty? It's salt beef." Hannah's face was incredulous. "It's stringy. Gets caught in my teeth. I hate the stuff."

You wouldn't know but he confessed to the worst crime in the universe. He could've said, "I just ran over Aunt Ida and left her for dead in a ditch." The reaction would've been the same.

Okay. Maybe that was a stretch. But they were talking about beef. Salt beef.

"Fine. I'll try it again. For you." And then, because if he was going to eat a heart attack on a plate for her, he was getting some satisfaction from it.

Leaning in, he planted a soft kiss on her soft pink lips.

"For you." It bore repeating. Then he looked at Fiona and Dillon and raised a finger. "Not a word. Not. One. Word. It's her Christmas and mine. You have something to say, we'll talk about it tomorrow."

Then for good measure, he put two pieces of salt beef on his plate and winked at Hannah. "If I die before I'm sixty, you can pinpoint this moment as the beginning of the end."

Hannah felt her face go from the normal heat of being in Toby's proximity to a whole new level of blushing. Refusing to look her sister in the eye, she grabbed another piece of beef and followed Toby into the dining room.

She felt a soft tug on her arm, clearly Fiona trying to pull her aside. Hannah shrugged her off and sat next to Toby.

"You're cracked," she whispered to Toby, unable to wipe an ever-widening smile from her face.

"About you," he said.

Her smile widened.

"Come on, Fiona," her mother called. "You can say grace."

Fiona took the seat across from Hannah. The look of questioning in her older sister's eyes was writ large. Hannah doubted Toby's edict to wait until tomorrow to talk about this was likely to happen.

Fiona cleared her throat. "Mom, I haven't said grace in so long, I don't even remember it."

"I'll do it." Hannah wasn't often the one to jump in and say the blessing, but right now she'd say anything to get the meal going.

A blaring series of honks that sounded like the air horns of a transport truck filled the room.

"What in the world is that?" Hannah's dad was the first to leave the table and go to the window.

"It's Grace!" Hannah's mother shrieked, and nearly knocked Hannah to the ground in her race to get to the door.

Sure enough, the middle Nolan daughter sat in the passenger side of an enormous Hummer. Not one of the newer models you saw around town. This was an honest-to-goodness Humvee, the kind you'd expect to see racing across some desert battlefield.

"Where in the name of God did they get that?" Dillon said, not moving from the window.

Only Toby remained at the table. Hannah wrapped her

arms around his shoulders. "We're all home for Christmas. There's nothing that could make this day better." She planted a kiss on his cheek and turned back to the window.

Asher exited the monstrous vehicle with a kind of cool saunter that only a bona fide rock star could pull off. He was certainly dressed for the weather, in jeans, kamicks, and a black puffy parka that was down-filled. He walked around the truck, if one could get away with calling a Hummer a truck, and helped Grace down.

In the two months since Grace had left to tour the world with Asher, nothing had changed about her appearance. Hannah had thought maybe Asher would encourage Grace to embrace a more hip look. But her sister was rocking the same brown ponytail and fresh-faced look that she'd sported in October, when she and Asher had fallen head over heels for each other.

The only noticeable difference in her sister was the way she looked up instead of down, facing the world rather than hiding from it. There was a visible change in the confidence her sister projected. And it made all the difference.

The house exploded once Grace and Asher entered. The dogs lost their minds. And so did her parents. Hugs and kisses and welcome-homes were doled out in frantic measure, as if they expected Asher to swoop Grace right back out the door.

Dillon and Toby were sent to the basement to bring up two more chairs while Hannah set out two extra places.

By the time they all sat down to dinner once again, the house was louder and more joyous than before.

"If I'd known my offering to say grace would've brought you here," Hannah said, "I would've done so yesterday."

As they ate, Grace explained the lengths Ted—Asher's real name, which Grace demanded they call him—had gone to in order to bring her home for Christmas.

"She was heartbroken," he said between mouthfuls of dinner. "As soon as there was a break in the weather, we took off. But we had to land in Gander because the snow was on track to hit hard again."

"We saw the Hummer sitting on the tarmac in Gander," Grace said. "Ted found the owner and made a very generous offer to rent it."

"I've never driven in such treacherous conditions in all my life. If this is winter in Newfoundland, we might be stuck here for some time. Because I don't think I'm driving in this ever again."

Hannah thought it was cute how Ted and Grace could tell a story in such a back-and-forth manner. It was clear their connection was solid and real. She hoped her mother noticed as well.

"You're welcome here, Ted," Hannah's dad said. "You can stay as long as you like, and you don't have to pay a fortune for a room up at the inn, either. Our house is your house any time you're in Heart's Ease."

Hannah wasn't certain if anyone else saw the look her dad shot her mom, but she did. It was a look that said, *He brought our little girl home for Christmas. He's good.*

It didn't seem like the look was necessary. Since Ted

walked in the door, her mother had fawned over him and Grace in equal measure.

The rest of dinner was spent with Grace regaling the whole family with tales of all the cities she'd visited, all the ways she'd fought with the paparazzi to protect Ted's privacy, and seemingly more important to her, the new job she'd acquired. Grace was always a geek at heart, and she'd just landed a job to work on a new video game that was going to turn the role-playing world on its axis.

After everyone had eaten their obligatory second plate of food, three for Dillon and, inexplicably given his size, four for Ted, her mom announced it was time for dessert.

A series of groans filled the room.

"How about me and Dillon and Ted do the dishes first," Toby said, standing and starting to collect the plates. "By then we'll have room to finish every bit of whatever feast you have in store for us."

If Toby's intention was to leap to the head of the pack of men vying for the status of favoured boyfriend, Hannah figured he had just managed to tie with Ted. And given that Ted had delivered Grace in a snowstorm, that was no small feat.

TWELVE

&

So many times in her past Hannah had wished her sisters were a larger part of her life. There was a warmth that came from being together, and she didn't care how much they teased her or made her feel like a baby, she would always choose being with Grace and Fiona over being alone.

"Oh my God," Fiona said, her groan deep and tortured. "Where does Mom find this fabric?"

"The Internet has made finding the most overly gaudy Christmas flannel a sport for Mom. I swear she starts shopping in January to find this stuff." Hannah pulled the ruffled flannel nightgown over her head. The one good thing about the nighties her mom made was that she was a stickler for comfort. No unwashed, starchy flannel for her girls. These gowns had been washed probably a dozen times, so they were soft and warm and comfortable. Dog ugly, but heaven on the skin.

This year's pattern was a series of gold and red poinsettias, clustered in a chintz design with a hunter green background. Elaborate ruffled necklines, hems, and cuffs showed that their mom had learned some new techniques.

"Let's all do our hair the same."

"Are you drunk, Grace?" Hannah thought this was the most un-Grace sentence ever uttered.

"No. I just thought Mom is so intent on re-creating our childhood that we might as well give her the picture-perfect moment she wants. Honestly, how many more Christmases do you think we're all going to be together?"

"What are you talking about?" Fiona said.

"Come on, Fiona. At some point you and Dillon are going to get married, have kids, and Christmas will become about them. And who knows where I'll be next Christmas? Ted can't always save the day and get me here. Plus, the idea of spending Christmas on the beach in Tahiti is pretty appealing right now. What about you?"

Grace looked at Hannah. "Where are you gonna go when you're finished your degree? Grad school? Travel the world? The point is, we shouldn't take this Christmas for granted. So if Mom wants us all dolled up in these nightgowns that she clearly put a lot of effort into, then we should smile and be happy and give her what she wants."

That was Grace in a nutshell. Kind, considerate, and logical.

Which is why, fifteen minutes later, the three Nolan girls joined their parents and boyfriends in the living room for trifle and tea, with their hair in messy buns, chignons, as Grace called them, wearing their mother's Christmas nightgowns.

"You're a vision," Mrs. Nolan said. "Stand there in front of the tree and I'll get a picture."

After a bit too much voguing for Gail's liking, she finally settled and proclaimed that there had to be at least one usable picture in the hundreds she clicked off on her iPad.

"Now, let's get the boys in there," Gail said.

Dillon and Ted jumped to their feet standing behind Fiona and Grace. Toby didn't move. Hannah's heart felt heavy.

"You too, Toby," her mom said. "Get in there. You and Hannah might not know what you're doing, but mark my words, you'll be back here with us next Christmas."

As Toby took his place next to her, Hannah forced a smile. Was Toby getting cold feet? Had Dillon said something to him while they were cleaning up?

"For the love of God, Gail, don't share this picture on Facebook," her father said. "Elsie's inn will be stuffed to the gills with young girls expecting to fall in love in Heart's Ease."

"You are a fine-looking group of young people," her mother agreed.

"Mom, please don't share this picture with anyone until Ted and I have left. We could use the privacy." Hannah noticed Grace take Ted's hand.

"Forget later. Don't ever share this with anyone. I mean, I know you like these granny gowns, Mom, but please, let's keep our Christmas jammies in the family?" Fiona flopped onto the sofa. "I have to represent some of the people who'll see this in court."

"Don't be so melodramatic, girls," her mother snipped as she laid the iPad on the coffee table.

Always the peacemaker, her dad jumped in, clapping his hands and sitting under the tree.

"I don't know about you, but I've been waiting all day to open some presents." He started handing out small packages to each of the girls.

"They might seem ladylike to you now," Dad said to the guys, "but you should have been around the year Grace's stack of gifts took up more room than Fiona and Hannah's combined."

"In my defence, I was thirteen. Hormones were to blame," Fiona said, burying her face in her hands.

Hannah started to laugh. "I didn't even notice."

"That's because you were still so young that no one bothered to wrap your presents. You came downstairs, saw a Barbie Dream House, and tuned out the world," Fiona said.

"Oh my God, I'd forgotten about that Christmas," Grace said, starting to laugh.

"That's likely the result of your concussion," Hannah said. "Fiona gave you a pretty big smack."

"I did not hit her!" Fiona said.

"Well, not with your body."

"You're not helping, Hannah." Fiona turned to Grace. "I didn't hit you on purpose."

"Before we have a repeat," her father said, "Grace asked for a few board games that year. And Fiona asked for jewellery. We like to spend the same on all the girls, so to make up for the ring and chain and earrings that Fiona got, Hannah got a lot of Barbies and doll clothes, and Grace got a lot of games. We noticed Christmas Eve how much bigger Grace's pile was, but figured it wouldn't be a problem."

"It was a problem," their mother said.

"It didn't help that you put my gifts in my stocking, so it looked like I had nothing under the tree." Fiona folded her arms, looking for all the world like the petulant preteen she was when the story was a reality.

"I can still remember you pulling out deodorant and candy and a toothbrush, looking under the tree, wondering what was yours."

Her mother started to laugh. "I'm sorry, sweetheart. It's not funny, and we learned a very valuable lesson that year about quantity versus value. But now that we're all older, surely we can laugh about it."

"It makes me seem like I was a brat," Fiona said.

Hannah wrapped an arm around her sister. "I was the brat. You were the perfect one. I think it's okay that you have one bad story. And I still love you."

"So do I," Grace said. "And I'm the one you whacked in the head with Hannah's Bop-it."

"I didn't do it on purpose. I was just tossing another present to my baby sister, and your head got in the way."

"Needless to say," Dan Nolan said. "It was quite the Christmas morning, and it took some ego-soothing to calm down a young teenager who learned a valuable lesson about getting what you asked for."

"Yeah, I'll be sure to remember it when I have kids," Grace said.

Hannah watched as Ted turned red. Something told her that was a bridge he wasn't quite ready to consider crossing yet. She'd have to get Grace alone while they were all home and see how serious things were between them. She didn't want Grace getting hurt if Ted wasn't on the same page as her sister.

Before long there was a nice little pile of presents gathered by Hannah's feet. Funky leggings and sweaters from her sisters, earrings from Dillon, which she knew Fiona had picked out, and a case of wine from Ted. There was no point in telling him it was too extravagant a gift. She didn't know him well, but figured he didn't consider cost when picking out a gift.

But it was her parents who delivered the best gift of all.

"We loved our cruise so much," her mom said, handing the girls small gift boxes. "But more often than not, we found ourselves wishing you were with us. So the next time we go, we are all going."

Inside the boxes were tiny cruise ships, sand, and shells.

"All we ask is that you figure out a seven-day window that works for all of you sometime this year. That can be your present to us."

Grace laughed as she handed her parents an envelope that read *To Mom and Dad, Love your girls*. "Well, that takes the shock value out of our present."

"We could tell how much you enjoyed your cruise, so we all chipped in and got you both another," Fiona said.

"It's too much," her father said, shaking his head. "Especially for you, Hannah."

Hannah hated this gift. Fiona and Grace were all for it, so she went along in the end, but they all knew her contribution was marginal. They'd assured her she didn't have to chip in a cent, that it would still be from all three of them, but it was beside the point.

Which is why she'd had no trouble breaking her word and wrapping another present. It wasn't like it cost her much. Yet.

"Don't worry about it, Dad. It's more from them than me. My bank account is okay. But I do have something for you."

"Hannah," Fiona said, giving her a scolding glare.

"It's something personal from me," she said, returning the look in full measure.

She handed the gift to her father.

"A study guide for the MCAT?" He stared at her.

"I was thinking you could help me study to get into med school."

"Med school?" her mother echoed.

"Yup, I've decided to be the next Dr. Nolan."

Hannah expected her father to be happy, but she hadn't anticipated the joy that erupted from her sisters and mother.

"About time you figured out what the rest of us knew," Grace said. "You were always going to be the one to follow in Dad's footsteps."

Hannah wasn't sure about that. Either Fiona or Grace could have become doctors. They were smart enough, that was certain. But she realized they followed their hearts. And so was she. It was the important part of her decision. She wasn't doing it for her father. She was doing it for her.

"I might not get into the school here," she said. "I might have to go away. I might not get accepted anywhere. But I'm going to try."

"Oh, you'll get into MUN," her father said. "Pass the test, write the best application letter you can, and I bet you'll ace the interview."

She was relieved he hadn't said he'd make sure of it. The last thing she wanted was him calling in favours. She had to do it on her own. She would do it on her own.

Before she could tell her father that, a loud banging on the door made her jump. She heard the porch door open, and then laughed in glee when a chorus of rough voices shouted, "Any mummers allowed in?"

THIRTEEN

This had to be a fire hazard. Kerosene lamps, candles, four bottles of rum spread out on the table, three guitars, an accordion, and at least a dozen people stomping and swinging their way around the kitchen.

Mummering was a grand old tradition. Hannah had never known for them to show up on Christmas night, but given the weather and the state of things in Heart's Ease, it wasn't surprising. Chances were that more than one family was going stir crazy in the dark.

Part of the fun of mummering was trying to figure out who was who, and Hannah was willing to bet there was at least one Walsh, one Nolan, and one O'Dea in the mix.

"Come on, me lover, how about a Christmas kiss?"

"You can change your voice as much as you want, Michael Nolan, but you're not fooling me." Hannah laughed. Mike was a few years older than her, and she knew he had no romantic interest in her, but it had never stopped them from flirting. It was one of those flirtations based on nothing more than friendship.

Mike pulled the pillowcase that was masking his face up just a fraction enough to show his cheek.

"Just a small one?"

"Not a chance." Instead, she patted his cheek and pulled the pillowcase back down.

"A jig it is, then." He grabbed her hand in his, which was sporting a pair of flowery pink rubber gloves, and pulled her into a two-step.

The mummers had arrived with one guitar, but luck was on their side. Maybe that's why they tried the Nolan house in the first place. Asher and Dillon had quickly grabbed their guitars, and Poppy Nolan had picked up the accordion.

Once the tune was over and Hannah had untangled herself from Mike, she made her way to Toby, who was deep in conversation with Grace.

"Isn't it wonderful to see Poppy having such a great time?" Hannah said.

"I'm so glad I'm home for Christmas," Grace said.

"You're lucky, the both of you, to have your grandfather in such good shape. You really should try and spend as much time with him as you can. You never know when things can change."

Toby's sage observation reminded Hannah that he had no family to spend Christmas with, and hadn't for a long time. She watched him through the day, noticing when he would let his guard down, and when he put it back up. There were layers to Toby that she would have to unpeel slowly.

She refused to let him wallow. Taking his hand, she led him into the thick of the dancing crowd. She knew he was a fine hand at a two-step. Up until yesterday, it was one of the few excuses she had to touch him.

Even though it must've been thirty degrees in the kitchen, her temperature rose in his arms.

He pulled her closer, and she could feel his breath on the side of her face. This was the first time in hours that they touched more than in passing. Her body reacted. All the longing she felt last night and this morning came back in a rush.

He slid his arm around her waist and pressed her to him. It was a subtle gesture that no one would notice. Hell, who could notice anything in this crowd? But she knew. She felt it. He wanted her as much as she wanted him.

She slid her hand that was at his shoulder across the back of his neck, where she could tease him At the point where his hair and neck met. She felt him shudder.

There was nothing she could say that wouldn't be overheard by someone, so any message she wanted to convey had to be done with her body.

It seemed he had the same idea.

As they danced, he pressed harder against her, leading her from the middle of the kitchen floor, closer to the door that led to the living room and dining room.

The table in the dining room had been quickly pushed

against the wall after the mummers had arrived. There was an odd assortment of dancers in there as well. One wearing a pair of nylons over her face nodded to Hannah. It was hard to tell, but she thought it might be Violet Walsh. There wasn't a family member in sight.

Hannah assumed control, waltzing Toby into the living room, where one lone mummer sat watching hockey.

"How are ya?" he said, his voice muffled through the lampshade on his head.

"Best kind," she said. "You know, you can take that off, if you want."

"Nah. Ruins the outfit."

Any another time, Hannah might have stopped to comment on that, but there were more pressing matters on her mind. One pressing matter, anyway.

She stopped dancing and took Toby's hand.

"Come on."

She led him upstairs.

"And where are you taking me?"

"Mom has rules about sharing rooms with boys, so you and Ted will be roommates tonight. I thought I'd show you to your quarters."

"So I'm a boy?"

"In her eyes, you're most likely a dangerous man intent on deflowering her virginal daughter."

"I'm not touching that comment. Mainly because I want to touch you."

"Smart man, on both counts."

She led him into her room. It was bigger than Grace's and could fit an air mattress on the floor.

" I suggest you go to bed before Ted or you will wind up on the floor."

"Stop talking."

The force of his words stopped her.

"Excuse me?"

"You heard me."

He closed the door and pushed her against it. Her heart raced. There was a new tension in the air. A feeling came over her that was hard to define.

Toby pinned her arms above her head, holding them in place with one hand.

She opened her mouth, but he pushed a finger against her lips.

"Shhh."

He moved his finger and covered her mouth with his.

He only touched her in two places; her mouth and her hands. But those touches were enough for her to recognize the feeling coursing through her was lust.

Not any lust. Not the juvenile kind of desire that you get when you're about to have your first kiss, or the first time a boy reaches his hands under your shirt. And not the sort of lust that comes over you when it's been too long between men and you'll take anything that piques your interest. No. This was a lust built on longing. A lust for one person, and one person only. A burning need flared between them, and the only thing that could control it was allowing the fire free rein.

She opened her mouth, inviting him deeper. He took her offer, and then trailed his mouth to her ear, her neck, and back to her lips.

Devoured. It wasn't a word she'd ever taken seriously. But this kiss? This was a devouring kiss.

His body pressed firmer against her. She tried to free her hands. She was used to being in control. Submitting wasn't in her DNA.

Stop, her subconscious hollered at her. *This is hot.*

"The bed is four steps away," she managed to say in stops and starts.

"I told you last night. There's no bed for us yet. And I'm not making love to you for the first time in your parents' house. Now stop talking. We'll be missed before long."

This new side of Toby was even more of a turn-on than all her fantasies of him. She'd imagined he'd be a slow se-ducer. Certainly last night had given that indication. But this side? This raw, I-need-you-now side was guaranteed to give her a sleepless night. Nights. Who knew when they'd be home again?

That idea made her shut her brain off and let her body enjoy every shiver, tingle, and tremor.

She wasn't certain when he let her hands go. Maybe he possessed some innate radar that told him when he'd kissed her into surrender.

Hell, she wouldn't have known except she jumped when one warm hand slid behind her, cupping her ass. His other hand remained behind her neck.

"Hannah? Toby?"

The door pushed against her, causing Toby to stagger as she fell against him.

Shit. Fiona.

FOURTEEN

‰

Thanks be to Jesus Toby hadn't let Hannah talk him into moving to the bed. The temptation was there. But he had enough sense to know that getting caught screwing the baby of the family on Christmas night, in her sweet teenage bed, no less, wouldn't have done either of them any favours.

He quickly flipped on the light as Fiona pushed her way into the room.

"Seriously?" she said. "What the hell is going on here?"

"If you have to ask, then you're clearly not as smart as I always figured you to be," Hannah said, standing closer to him.

Toby loved Hannah's smart mouth, but he didn't think it was going do either of them any favours in subduing Fiona's irritation.

"What did I tell you?" Fiona seemingly ignored Hannah and directed her fury at him.

He didn't care. Fiona could exhaust her red-headed anger, and then he'd speak. He'd watched her and Dillon fight enough times that he'd figured out how to deal with her.

Hannah, however, didn't seem to know this.

"What right did you have telling him anything? Least of all anything to do with me? I'm not a baby to be protected. And I certainly don't appreciate you playing judge, jury, and executioner in my love life."

It was cute the way she stepped in front of him. Cute. But not necessary.

"I—" Fiona's words were cut off.

"Did I interfere with you and Dillon? I gave you a heads-up so you'd know what to expect when you came home. But I was always supportive of you. With Mom. With half the harbour. I had your back. I didn't go behind your back and warn him away."

"That's different, Hannah."

"Really? Different how?"

"Because you're younger than I am. You haven't had enough experience to be able to deal with a reckless fling."

"You don't know the first thing about my experiences. Since you've been home, everything has been about you and your issues with Dillon. And then Grace and Asher. Who, I'd like to point out, you were more than supportive of."

"Look, I think Toby is great." She looked at him. "I do. I think you're awesome. But admit it. You go through women pretty damn fast."

"Oh, you mean since Dillon no longer wants them?" Hannah marched to the door and opened it. "You don't know anything about anything. I'm pissed at you, Fiona. And I want to have a rip-roaring fight with you. But I'm not going to ruin Christmas by having this out now. I'm not going to do it to Mom. So you have two choices. Accept the fact that me and Toby are together, or shut up and simmer over it at your own pace."

"Don't walk out of this room until I've had my say," Fiona said, reaching to close the door.

"Oh, I'm not leaving. You are. I was in the middle of kissing my boyfriend. And I'm going to kiss him again until the only reason I can't catch my breath is because he kissed me senseless. Again."

Turned out Hannah knew exactly how to calm the beast.

"Your boyfriend?"

Toby felt an unexpected rush of heat in his cheeks. But yeah, why not?

"I wouldn't mess around with Hannah. I care too much about her for that. I get why you told me to stay away. Once Dillon went off the market, I had a couple of great months. But that's not my style. I'm not a one-night-stand guy." Fiona's face turned scarlet. "Not that Dillon was," he said, although it was a lie. Before Fiona, Dillon was the quintessential one-night-stand guy. But he was trying to get her calm, not make matters worse.

Fiona dropped onto the bed. Crap. Was she settling in for a play-by-play?

"How long has this been going on? Why didn't you tell me?"

Toby got the feeling this wasn't directed at him. He was torn between leaving them to do whatever it was girls did when they talked about the guys in their lives, or staying in case things escalated and a referee was needed.

If Hannah sat beside Fiona, he'd take that as a cue to go. But if she stayed beside him, he'd stay.

"I'll tell you everything, if you promise to be civil and supportive."

"Mom sent me up to make sure there's no bloodshed," Grace said from out in the hall. Toby couldn't imagine growing up in a house full of people with nowhere to go for escape. Then again, it wasn't likely any of the Nolans had a true reason to hide away as kids.

She stuck her head into the room. "But what I need to know is why there would be bloodshed in the first place."

"You're just in time," Fiona said, scooting farther back onto the bed.

"For what?"

"For the story of how Toby became Hannah's boyfriend."

Grace squealed. It figured. He was familiar with squealing girls. It happened the few times Asher had played at the bar.

"I'm so glad I made it home," she said, joining her sisters on the bed.

This was definitely his cue to leave.

"Toby," Fiona called out, just as he'd left the room.

"Yeah?"

"Have fun telling Dillon. It was his rule, you know. Not mine."

⊷

About forty minutes later, the mummers decided to clear out and let the Nolans get back to their Christmas. The girls hadn't come downstairs. At some point their mother had disappeared as well.

How much of yesterday would Hannah share with them? Everything? A little? How much detail? Was she up there right now reciting word for word every little detail? She could. She had an incredible memory and ability to play back conversations.

They'd need to have a talk about boundaries.

"You're not tending bar tonight," Dan Nolan told him, snapping him out of his reverie.

Hannah's dad nodded to the handful of beer bottles Toby was stacking in a case.

"I've been watching you all night. As soon as an empty glass or bottle touched the counter or table, you were Johnny-on-the-spot, picking it up."

"It's habit," Toby said, carrying the beer case to the porch.

"Gail noticed it earlier. Her pet peeve is cleaning up after a time. She can't stand waking in the morning and having to face a mess of empties and sink full of glasses."

"When I was a kid, I decided I didn't have to eat my cereal

with a table full of bottles surrounding me. I learned to pick them up as I saw them empty."

Where had that come from? It was too easy in this house to let his guard down.

He cleared his throat and bent to pull on his boots. "I'll go bring in some more wood."

Then he remembered Fiona's last words.

"Come on, Dillon," he said. "We'll make short work of filling up the woodbox."

The latest squall had blown over, and while it wasn't a clear night, at least there wasn't snow blowing in his eyes. He beat down the new snow with his boots as he walked to the woodshed.

From behind, Dillon shone a flashlight up the path.

"Did you notice Fiona and her sisters have disappeared?" Dillon said.

"Oh yeah," Toby said.

"I wonder if she's planning on staying here tonight? You know, you're welcome to come back to Mom's with me. Likely be more comfortable for you that the sofa is there. Should ask Asher, too."

"Ted," Toby said, starting to load his arms with wood.

"Yeah. I don't know if I'll ever get used to that. It would be like meeting Beyoncé and she asked to be called Sue."

Toby laughed.

"Your mother's house is smaller than this one. And I'm thinking I'd end up on the sofa there as well. Can't get over to your place tonight?"

"God, no. Can't take the boat in this."

"I'll stay put, then. Besides, I think Hannah wants me to stay."

He waited for Dillon to say something. Instead, all he heard was the soft clunk of wood knocking wood as Dillon piled a load into the crook of his arm.

"Something happened yesterday. With us. Me and Hannah."

"I figured."

"You did?"

"You're here. It's Christmas. You're not moping. And then there was the salt beef kiss."

"Right." He'd forgotten about that.

"I figured you'd tell me when you were good and ready. Clearly you're not just sleeping with her, or you wouldn't be here. I'm taking your presence as a sign that this is more than sex."

"It's more than sex." He hesitated. "Christ, Dillon. There's been no sex at all. It only started yesterday."

"I don't need the details."

"I don't intend to give them to you. But." he laid down the couple pieces of wood he'd grabbed and sat on the woodpile. "Sit down, will ya? I need to talk."

Dillon dropped his armful of wood and sat.

"It's the damnedest thing," Toby said after a moment. "I've been attracted to her for a long time. A couple of years, at least. And then we moved in together, and you and Fiona laid down the law, and I tried, buddy. I tried hard to not do anything about it. But it made things worse."

Dillon said nothing. Just leaned back farther and crossed his arms. Classic listening position for his friend.

"It went from a physical attraction to getting to know her. To care for her. It made it harder. And yesterday, well, it all came to a head. And for some reason, she feels the same."

"I know."

"What do you mean, you know?"

"I know how you feel about her."

"Since when?"

"Since the last time I was in town and I watched the two of you. I said to Fiona, it's only a matter of time before the two of them figure out that they don't hate each other. And then they're going to love each other with the same intensity."

There it was again. That unspoken word that had hung around him like a haze since he'd first thought it earlier today.

"It's too soon for love."

"It might be too soon to admit it out loud. But you're on the road, my friend. I see it. I know you. I know you don't put yourself in situations where you're not in control. And you have no control over what happens when you're surrounded by Nolans. You're here because of her. And you'll stay because of her."

"So you're not pissed off that I broke your rule?"

Dillon laughed. "That rule was invented to force you to come to grips with your feelings about Hannah before you did something stupid like jump into bed with her the second night you were in the same house."

"I wouldn't have."

Dillon stood and started packing up wood again.

Toby thought back to the first night he and Hannah were alone in the house. He'd passed her bedroom and the door was open a crack. She was sitting on the bed brushing her hair, in nothing but a black lace something or other. He'd been certain she knew he was there. He'd felt her silent invitation. He'd hesitated. If he opened the door, there'd be no leaving that room till morning. Instead, he'd reached out and pulled the door closed. It wasn't until he'd gotten to his room that he allowed himself to breathe.

Yeah. Dillon was right. He would have. And he'd have ruined everything.

FIFTEEN

ๅ

Hannah was the first one up on Boxing Day. She always was. When she was a kid, she'd been unable to stay in bed knowing there were so many toys under the tree still waiting to be properly admired. And when they'd moved to Heart's Ease, she'd gotten up because she was cold and decided to learn to start the fire. That was also the year she decided to cook breakfast for everyone. It had become her thing.

She pulled on a pair of wool socks and pulled a hoodie over her flannel nightie. Flipping the light switch to test for power, and being oddly elated that they were still living off the grid, she slipped out of the room, careful not to wake Grace or Fiona. Softly, she padded down the hall. She hesitated outside the room where Toby slept. Then kept going.

Downstairs, she was met by the soft whistle of the kettle and the sound of a crackling fire as someone stoked the wood.

Instinctively, she knew. She tightened her ponytail and went in to meet him.

Her good morning was on the tip of her lips, but before she could get it out, Toby dropped a kiss on the top of her head and pulled her into his arms.

"It's so quiet here when you're all asleep."

"You prefer it that way?"

"It's a nice way to ease into the day. But no. I think I prefer all the racket. I was tempted to go wake you up but didn't want to stir the others."

She stretched up and kissed him.

"You wanna help me make breakfast?"

It wasn't the question she wanted to ask. But she didn't want to find out just yet if he planned on hightailing it back to St. John's this morning so he could work.

She suspected he'd leave as soon as breakfast was over. She knew Toby. He wouldn't call Billy in to work if he was perfectly capable of doing it himself. But if the power was gone, he couldn't open regardless.

She hoped the blackout continued until tomorrow.

"How about we have a cup of tea first?"

While he poured the tea, she let the dogs in. Their black and white shaggy coats were covered in a dusting of snow. They must have been rolling around, since a clear blue sky with white fluffy clouds greeted her.

She rubbed them down with a towel as they jumped and clamoured for her affection.

"We should have a dog," Toby said as he laid the cups on the table.

"We should?"

"Yeah. Keep you company at night when I'm at work. Keep me company during the day when you're at school."

"You work night and day," she said, tucking her legs under her as she sat down.

"I've been working too much," he said. "This winter I'm going to talk to Dillon and see what he wants to do with the music shop."

"You don't want to work there?"

"It's not that. I love it there. But between that and the bar, I'd choose the Banshee. It makes more money."

"Your dad was an alcoholic, right?" She said it softly.

"Yeah." His body tensed. It was hard to see if you didn't know what to look for. The way his hand clenched the cup a little harder. The set of his jaw.

"And you own a bar."

"I do. It's not because of the booze. It's because of the music and the people. But you can't have a dry music venue. Not in this town. And I like to have a drink. But believe me, I'm aware of every drink I have." He picked up the can of milk and made the hole a little wider with the butter knife. "You think I don't wonder if I'm setting myself down Dad's path? If his genes run through me? But I'm not him. I know that. If I ever woke in the morning and my first thought was that I needed a drink to face the day, or if I found myself getting angry at the people I loved because I had to choose between them or a drink . . ."

"I didn't mean that," she said, guilt coursing through her. "Honestly. That's not where I was going. I guess I was trying to ask how you can handle being around drunk people so much. Doesn't it get to you?"

He laughed, and she felt a little better. She'd never wondered if he drank too much. She knew better. Hell, she drank more than he did.

"Wanna know the truth?"

More than anything. But she didn't say it.

"I love the power. How often have you seen someone leave the Banshee blind drunk? If it happens, its few and far between. I'm not out to make a fortune off of people's drinking. That's why my cover charge is high. I want people coming for the show. And I love refusing to serve someone who's clearly reached their limit. I do. I wish more bartenders had refused to serve my dad. I wish some of them had considered the shape he was in when he'd left. Thought about what he was going home to."

"You're the bartender you wish your dad had."

Sailor plopped his head on Toby's lap.

"Basically, yeah."

They sat in silence for a moment, savouring their tea. Suddenly, an ungodly racket filled the room. Beeps and whirs and a cacophony of all the countless things powered by electricity coming to life.

The peace was broken.

Toby reached into his pocket and pulled out his phone.

"Just in time," he said, holding the phone where she could see it. "Six per cent battery life left. But it's enough."

"For what?"

"To call Billy and tell him I won't be back in town for another day or so."

"What if he can't work?"

"Then I'll go back tomorrow. One day won't break the bank."

A sense of elation filled her. It was a small thing. But it was a big thing, too. He was making a choice. And he chose her.

Boxing Day went by in a blur. Between watching hockey, eating leftovers, and playing a bunch of board games, the day evaporated. Hannah had tried to get everyone to go mummering that evening, but Ted wanted to keep things low-key. "I haven't done a family Christmas in a long time," he'd said. "And I like this sitting around, eating till my pants bust, and basking in the glow of a Christmas tree. I think I could do this every year and not get tired of it." He didn't even go visit Elsie, Daphne, or Ida.

Dillon went to his mother's for a while, but he was at the Nolan house more often than not.

And Toby. Well, Hannah had never seen photos of Toby as a child. Didn't even know if they existed. But there was a boyishness to his contentment that make her heart flutter. This was her family. He was happy with them. With her. And she knew, deep in her gut, that being with them was doing something for his soul. Mending a part of him he likely didn't even know was broken.

Just after midnight, her father said good night.

"Be sure to put some wood in the stove before you go to bed," he said. "There's a chance we might lose power overnight."

The outage had been so severe that Newfoundland Power had brought on a series of rolling blackouts so people could warm up and get some food cooked. So far Heart's Ease had kept their power, but it was likely only a matter of time before they lost it again.

Once it was just her and Toby, she curled up next to him on the sofa.

"Long day." Hannah snuggled into a welcoming spot he made for her against his chest.

"Hard work doing nothing."

Her eyes fluttered closed as he gently stroked her hair.

"You weren't bored?"

"Nah. It was actually really welcoming. Your family is great. The hardest part of the day was wanting to spend some time with you alone. But we have plenty of that ahead of us."

"Do you think it's going to be weird?"

"What?"

"Home. When we go home again. Things will be different."

"The only thing that's going to be different once we're back at our place is that now when you drive me 'round the bend, I can kiss some sense into you."

"Oh, really? You think so? You think you can just kiss me and everything will be hunky-dory?"

"Probably not. But at least I'll get to kiss you."

His laugh shook her head against his chest.

"Promise me one thing?"

"Sweetheart, I'm not good with promises. But I'll try my best. What is it?"

She took a deep breath. "Don't cheat on me, okay? I can't handle that. If you meet someone, and there's a spark there, do me the courtesy of telling me first. Make a clean break of it?"

Hannah wasn't prepared for the sudden movement as Toby pushed her back into a sitting position.

He took her hands and kissed them. First one, then the other. And then he kissed her lips.

Her pulse quickened.

"Hannah, I'm not a cheater. Never have been. And I might be taking a risk in saying this, but from where I stand, there's no room for anyone else to spark anything. It would have to be a damn explosion for me to even notice another woman. Like a Big Bang–calibre explosion. And I don't see that happening."

"Why?"

"Why? Because that's how you rocked my universe. You came at me with all the force in the galaxy. And that kind of thing doesn't happen twice in any lifetime."

"Toby. I . . ."

No. She couldn't say it. Not yet. She knew she loved him. But she couldn't say it. They might have had feelings for each other for years, but they'd only allowed themselves to admit their feelings three days ago. Or was it two? How did you

123

count something like this? Whatever it was, she wouldn't ruin it by saying she loved him. Putting him on the spot. But she did. And when the time was right, she'd tell him.

Instead of finishing her sentence, she pulled him to her and kissed him. Kissed him the way he'd kissed her the night before. She pushed him onto his back and straddled his body.

He pulled his mouth away.

"What were you going to say?"

"I want to go back to town tomorrow. With you."

"Why? You'd planned to be out all week."

She shook her head. "I'm going back with you. There are two things I want to do." She peppered him with kisses again.

"What's the first thing?"

"I want to go visit your grandfather with you. For Christmas. Whatever's going on there, I want to be with you when you deal with it."

She wasn't sure how he'd take it, so she pushed ahead to the second part.

"And secondly, I want to do this. More of this. Much much more of this so I can convince you that more than kissing is the way to go."

Before he could answer, she slid her hands under his shirt and kissed him again.

"Deal?" she said when she finally came up for air.

"Deal," he said. "And sweetheart?"

"Yeah."

"For the record, that thing you were going to say and then changed your mind about?"

There was no way he knew what she'd been about to say. But she stayed silent.

"Me too, Hannah. Me too."

BONUS STORY:
A KISS WORTH CHASING

Surprise! It's a bonus Heart's Ease Christmas story! A short story on its own is too small for a print run. But thanks to Flanker Press and their encouragement to expand Hannah and Toby's story, I can now share with you *A Kiss Worth Chasing.*

Home alone for the holidays. Can Christmas get any worse for Ginny Winter? A disastrous run-in with a stranger who gifts her with a major case of insta-lust doesn't bode well. Neither does his relentless pursuit. What's he chasing? And will he get his prize?

A Kiss Worth Chasing

ONE
꙰

"Now don't forget to water my orchid. Just soak the whole pot in water for five minutes and then let it drain. Once a week."

"I know, Mom."

"And don't leave the food out for the cat all day. If she gains any more weight, her legs are gonna give out. Or she might drop dead of a stroke."

"I know, Mom."

Ginny Winter hefted her mother's huge stuffed-to-the-gills purse on her shoulder, grabbed the handle of the carry-on suitcase, and did a once-over of the WestJet check-in counter.

"Mom, your passport and boarding pass."

She nodded to the documents still sitting beside the scales where she'd just paid for three overweight pieces of luggage.

For someone so intent on making sure Ginny remembered the ream of instructions for house-sitting, Dolores Winter couldn't manage to keep her travel papers in hand. So much for organizational skills.

Her mother grabbed the documents and passed her daughter. "Virginia, keep up. I need to get through security."

Not soon enough, Ginny thought.

"You're sure you can't come?" her mother continued. "Mark said he'd be happy to pay for your ticket, too."

"I wish," Ginny said, not meaning it in the slightest. "But I have to work."

"Laura could have watched the shop. She takes advantage of you because you don't have children."

Ginny rolled her eyes. This again.

"Mom, Laura is working, too. It's two days till Christmas. Everyone is working."

Never mind she wasn't actually needed at the shop. She'd told her mother she couldn't possibly go because she had a slew of last-minute orders to make up. After all, a good chunk of her stock was depleted when Mark had invited them to Houston for Christmas. Helen, her sister-in-law, had decided to give all of her friends Ginny's croched scarves for Christmas. It accounted for part of the bulk going with her mother.

But she had enough stock to get through the Christmas rush. It was more a matter of stubbornness and not wanting to pack up and go to Texas. There was no chance of a white Christmas in Houston. Plus, she was thirty-three years old. It was a grown-up thing to do to spend Christmas alone.

"I still think it's terrible to leave you behind for Christmas."

Personally, Ginny thought it was terrible of Mark and Helen to cancel their trip home days before Christmas and expect Mom to fly down instead. If they'd planned it earlier, then she would have understood. But apparently the oil industry might collapse if Mark dared leave Texas for two weeks. Who knew her brother was that important?

"Don't worry about me. I'll be fine. I'm going to Laura's for dinner. And Daniel is having a Tibb's Eve party tonight."

That was sure to keep her hungover throughout Christmas Eve.

"Daniel," her mother snorted. "You should stay home out of it. You've wasted enough of your time on him. He was never good enough for you. All he does is make you doubt yourself. The man should pay you, the way he treats you like you're his personal errand girl. And you. Foolish enough to still give him the time of day. Friendship is a two-way street, my darling. And he repaved that into a dead-end, one-way road a long time ago."

Ginny groaned. Her mother was in good form today.

Thanks be to Jesus the escalator to security was ahead.

She handed her mother the purse and bag and gave her a hug.

"Have a great trip, Mom. Love you."

Her mother hugged her back.

"I'll miss you. Be a good girl."

Be a good girl. That was Ginny's problem. She'd spent her life listening to her mother, and the command to be a "good girl" every time she left the house had ingrained itself into her.

She'd never been a bad girl. Didn't know how. Perhaps if she were less of a good girl, she wouldn't have pined after stupid, dense Daniel Caddigan for half her life—even after he'd dumped her.

Pulling her scarf loose, she waved at her mother and turned to leave.

"Excuse me."

A devastatingly delicious-smelling man pushed past her, knocking her against the rail of the escalator.

Figured. She was practically invisible to the opposite sex. Then he stopped. Turned.

"I'm sorry."

He made actual eye contact when he said it. How rare. Almost as rare as the steel-blue eye colour she couldn't tear her eyes away from. He stared at her intensely. Did she have something on her face?

"No problem," she said, before a jerk of her head followed by a constriction around her neck as her jade scarf tightened and cut off any further conversation. She clutched at her throat and did a spin, trying to loosen the grip the delicate scarf made as it was carried up the escalator.

"Shit! Don't move," he said, a bit calmer than she would have anticipated.

But she had to move or she was going to be killed by her own creation.

Amid her scrambling and spinning, she saw him sprint up the stairs and rip out the tiny strand of the scarf that had gotten stuck in the handrail.

The grip around her neck didn't exactly loosen itself, but it did stop its murderous plot, which was all she needed.

Fumbling, she pulled off the scarf. It wasn't completely ruined. But the work it would take to fix it again wasn't worth it. That was too bad. It was the first in this pattern she'd made and she loved it, rookie mistakes and all.

"That was a close one," said a deep voice with just the faintest hint of a townie twang to it. "Does adventure always follow you around?"

She wasn't sure if she should think of him as her rescuer or the scarf's murderous accomplice.

Gratitude won out.

"Thanks for your help," she said, trying not to stare too much. This guy was off-the-charts on the sexy man scale. A grey wool suit jacket over a white shirt with a hint of a grey T-shirt underneath. It wasn't hard to imagine that it clung to a perfectly sculpted body that was likely flawless. Trying her best to subtly scan his body downward, she wasn't shocked to find that instead of dressing the look down with jeans, he'd taken it to another level in charcoal pants with the slightest grey pinstripes.

She gulped. Yes. Literally. Gulped at the gorgeousness in front of her.

"Are you all right?" His stare made her uncomfortable. "You seem a little . . ."

Thank God he thought her loopiness was caused by near-strangulation and not a case of insta-lust.

"Sorry," she said, knotting the scarf in her hands and setting her eyes firmly on the wall behind him. It wasn't possible to look at him and talk at the same time. "I'm fine. Really. Thanks for your help."

She'd already said that. Why couldn't she think of something cute and flirty to say? Why did she have to feel heat coursing to her face and dryness in her throat?

"Are you sure? Why don't you sit down for a minute and I'll go get you something to drink?"

"No, no. I'm fine. Honestly."

Her throat was burning. She rubbed it.

"Let me see," he said, stepping even closer.

Breathe, she commanded herself.

The shock to her skin when he reached out and tilted her chin upward with his hand was nearly her undoing. No man had ever touched her this way.

Even in her short relationship with Daniel, which was mainly about pity-sex for him and a need to pretend it was about more for her. Daniel had touched her plenty. But never in a way that felt so invasively tantalizing. And it was just her chin, for God's sake.

"Your neck is red," he said. "I wouldn't be surprised if it bruises a little. That was a close call."

The serious set of his eyes brought home the realization that she could have been hurt very badly had he not been there to help.

"Come on," he said, taking her by the arm and leading her to one of the lines of chairs that ran the length of the airport. "Sit down for a minute."

He reached into his bag and pulled out a bottle of water. Then hesitated.

"I've drunk from it," he said, apologetically. "I'll go get another."

"Are you sick?" Did she really say that?

"Other than a self-induced hangover, no."

She reached out and took the bottle. The need to drink overtook all else.

"Are you a doctor?"

He had to be. Or maybe a male nurse? Someone who had compassion for poor helpless souls. No way. There was no way he was a nurse. Not that men couldn't be nurses. But his clothes shouted expensive. That jacket alone probably cost a paycheque of one of the Health Sciences Centre's finest.

He laughed. "No."

Not big on conversation, was he?

After chugging half the bottle of water, she handed it back to him.

"Keep it. You'll need it more than me."

He glanced at his watch and then clapped his hands together.

"Feeling better?"

This was it. Time for her brief dalliance with hotness to end. It was a five-minute span of life she'd remember forever.

She nodded. "Yes, thank you. You can go. I have to get to work."

"You're sure you're okay to drive?"

Rubbing her neck and twisting it a little, she realized she wasn't hurt that badly at all. A little stiff, but nothing major.

"Absolutely." Ginny stood.

Awkwardly, she stuck out her hand. Was a handshake the right way to thank someone for kindness? She wasn't sure.

"Thanks again. Have a good Christmas."

The glance he gave her hand was all the sign she needed to know it was just as weird as she'd thought.

"Please don't thank me. It's my fault it happened. I'm sorry I banged into you. I wasn't paying attention."

"Don't worry about it. I'm fine."

"Glad to hear it. Merry Christmas to you as well."

More awkward goodbyes, and she turned to go. In a normal world, that would have been the end of it. But destiny seemed unwilling to let her embarrassment pass.

Instead of walking briskly past her and on to whatever a GQ model did in St. John's for the holidays, he kept pace with her.

It felt like it was on purpose. His legs were a lot longer than hers. He should have passed her by now.

"Getting a cab?" he asked.

"No. I drove."

The back of her neck burned hot. Spontaneous chit-chat wasn't easy for her.

"Would you mind dropping me at the most convenient coffee shop? My ride is delayed, and I'd sooner not hang out here for the next few hours."

She did a mental recognizance of her car. The normal pile of takeout containers was resting in her mother's garbage after this morning's cleanup.

"Are you familiar with St. John's?"

He laughed. A rich, gruff sound that did something unexplainable to her stomach.

"I'm from here. I might not be up on the most recent changes, since I've lived away for a while. But I know my way around."

"In that case, I can drop you anywhere you want to go between here and Water Street."

"Oh, there's tons of places for me to kill time downtown. Just go where you're going and I'll be fine."

Fine. Not a word to adequately describe anything to do with this man.

Somehow she made it through the drive without acting like a total freak show. Then again, he did most of the talking. There wasn't much substance to the conversation, mainly observations about what had changed since his last visit five years ago. But she did get some basics. His name was Sean. He was a physiotherapist. He was spending Christmas around the bay with a friend. She was willing to bet that friend was female.

As she drove the length of Water Street twice in search of a parking spot, she finally stopped in front of Atlantic Place.

"I'm going to have to park a ways away. No need for you to suffer because of it."

"Tired of my company?"

A nervous laugh crept out of her. "No. You're much better company than the CBC." The truth was, she was going to go park at her house and then walk to the shop. Her street had a bad reputation. Her mother still wasn't done with the lecture about her buying a house on a street that was famous for slum landlords and a sensational murder. Gentrification was slowly happening, but he wouldn't know that.

"I should get that put on my card. Sean King. Better company than news radio."

There went that silly laugh of hers again.

He got out of the car and grabbed his suitcase.

"Thanks for the ride, Ginny. I'm glad you didn't do any serious damage to yourself."

"Nice to meet you, Sean. Enjoy your Christmas around the bay."

He shut the door, knocked on the window, and wagged his fingers goodbye. When he turned away, she let out a long exhale.

For a full minute she sat there watching him walk away. It wasn't until a loud honk behind her pulled her out of her thoughts that she drove away, lamenting that she hadn't said or done anything to make a lasting impression.

TWO
∽

"And you didn't even get his number?" Laura asked as she adjusted the clothesline display in the front window. She held up a pair of mittens in one hand and a hat in the other.

Ginny pointed to the mitts and continued crocheting a coffee cozy. She couldn't concentrate on a more complex pattern and bemoan her dismal performance as ingenue.

"What reason would I have for asking? 'Oh, hey. Can I have your number to store in my phone and never get the nerve to use?' I don't see that working."

"Nothing is going to work if you don't take the initiative."

"I never know what to say."

"Liar. You know what to say, only you won't let yourself do it. Be impulsive. Stop thinking about what you should do. Let your gut take over for a change."

"My gut? My gut tells me I'm going to make an idiot of myself."

"Fine. Your heart, then. Let your heart make some decisions for you."

It was so easy for Laura. Extroverts didn't understand the torrent of thoughts that raced through Ginny's introverted brain. She'd read a lot about it and was trying to be more outgoing. But it was hard to counteract a lifetime of shy over-contemplation.

She was trying to find a new way to describe her dilemma when the door opened.

Fate was out to get her.

"Sean."

Ginny stood and dropped her wool and hook.

His face was meant for smiling. It reached right to the fine lines at the corner of his eyes. "If it isn't the lovely Ms. Ginny. Glad to see you didn't take a turn for the worse."

Laura remained at the window, giving Ginny a face that proved that he truly was as sexy as she'd said.

"Still stranded in town?"

"Not quite stranded yet. I'm hoping to get a rental and drive myself. Waiting for one of the agencies to call me back. Figured I'd do some shopping while I waited."

"Are you looking for something for your wife?" Laura asked. It wasn't her normal salesperson mode. No. She knew her friend. This was Snooping 101.

"Unless you know something I don't, no," he said, briefly looking at Laura before turning back to Ginny, giving a wink that told her he knew exactly what her friend was up to.

"Actually, I noticed that scarf in the window and it reminded me of yours. I thought I should come in and warn the owner that they were selling a health hazard."

Ginny's face grew hot. Again. "I made that."

He laughed. "I was beginning to piece that together. I'm kidding. At least about the warning. I did notice the scarf, though, and thought it would make a nice present. It looked great on you before I ripped it."

"Any particular colour?"

"I have no idea. It's for my buddy's wife. I've never met her. Maybe the green you were wearing? If she's got honey-gold hair like yours, then I know it'll be great."

Honey gold? Who'd ever called her hair that shade? She was far more dirty blonde than honey gold. He was clearly a natural-born flirt. Not to mention he'd remembered the colour of her scarf.

"I'm out of that shade." Damn her sister-in-law. "But how about this silver-blue one? It goes good with all complexions."

Before he could reply, his cell rang.

She turned to give him privacy and locked eyes with Laura. There was a glow on her friend's face Ginny hadn't seen in a while. She mouthed something that Ginny couldn't make out.

It might have been *damn*.

Nope. She did it again.

Do him.

That couldn't be right.

Nope. She was right.

Do him.

Ginny walked away and took another scarf off the shelf, trying to ignore Laura and eavesdrop on Sean's call.

"You're kidding me. Seven hundred bucks for a car? For three days? Keep it."

He dropped the phone in his pocket and leaned against the counter in the middle of the store.

"Well, ladies. Any advice on finding a rental car from someone who's not a complete shyster?"

Laura's words echoed in Ginny's head.

Follow your gut.

"Where are you going?" she asked.

"Little place out on this side of Trinity Bay. Heart's Ease. I bet I could get a cab out there for less than that car would cost."

"I know where Heart's Ease is," Ginny said. There was an inn out there she'd always wanted to stay at. She'd booked a room once to surprise Daniel. Two days before they were supposed to go, he surprised her by dumping her. At least the inn was good enough to give her a refund. "It's less than a couple hours' drive. I could . . ."

Could what? The words stuck in her throat. Let them out, her brain screamed. What have you got to lose?

Deep breath. "I could drive you."

She could swear Laura let out a little yelp before she disappeared to the storeroom.

"I couldn't ask you to do that."

"You're not asking. I'm offering."

"It doesn't seem right."

"You had no trouble asking for a ride to a coffee shop." She laughed. A real laugh. An honest one. Not the nervous giggle that so often came out of her.

His eyes met hers. "You're serious? You'd drive me out?"

"I wouldn't have mentioned it if I weren't."

"I'll pay for the gas." He looked at his watch. "No. Forget it. It'll be close to dark when we get there. I don't want you driving back in the dark. I've almost killed you once today. Don't want to risk your life again."

An idea sprung to mind. What else did she have to do tonight? Go to a party at her ex's house, get drunk, and watch him drag off someone as equally opposed to commitment as he was?

"Tell you what. Let me call the Heart's Ease Inn. If I can get a room for the night, there'll be nothing to worry about."

She thought about her bank account. It was a bit of a splurge, but wouldn't it be great to wake up on Christmas Eve in a place she'd longed to visit?

"No way. You're not putting yourself out for me."

"I'm not putting myself out. I've always wanted to go there. This is the excuse I've needed."

So what if her daydreams of the inn included a generous helping of romance. She was a big girl. She could make it special on her own.

"You're sure?"

"She's sure," Laura yelled from the back room.

Rolling her eyes, Ginny gave God's gift to women her brightest smile.

"I'm sure."

Liar.

She was so not sure.

THREE

The ride to Heart's Ease wasn't quite perfect. For starters, they couldn't agree on what music to listen to. He was a classic country music guy. She didn't think men who wore designer clothes listened to George Jones. Turned out she was wrong.

Then there was the not-so-subtle suggestion that she drove too fast and there was no need to break the sound barrier to get rid of him. And there was the looming issue of not knowing if there was a room for her at the inn. Turned out Sean's friend's wife was the sister-in-law of the inn's owner and had promised to find Ginny a room even though the place was booked.

They hadn't heard from her in an hour.

"You're not stressed about the room, are you?" he asked, turning down Boney M's "Mary's Boy Child." For the last ten minutes the only sound in the car was their compromise choice of music.

"It's not a problem. If I don't get a room, I'll take my time and head home."

146

"No way. I can crash at Jack's place and you can take my room at the inn."

Her heart lurched. Sleep in his room? Even if he wasn't in it? That sounded like a terrible idea. Like something a woman who'd spent her life doing what was right and not at all scandalous would never, ever do.

Words failed her, so she shook her head.

"Disagree all you like, but I'm serious. I can be pretty convincing. I'll hide your keys if you try to drive back tonight. Look at that sky."

No need to point out the obvious. The sky was getting darker and darker, and it had nothing to do with the setting sun. Those clouds were about to erupt with snow.

The weather gods took Sean's side and decided it was time to let their Christmas decorating begin.

"If I say something along the lines of told you so, will you ever speak to me again?"

Ginny laughed in spite of herself. She'd done that a lot so far today.

The snow started falling quickly. In the few minutes remaining in their drive to Heart's Ease, the snow began to stick to the road.

There was no way she was getting home tonight.

"Have you been to Heart's Ease before?" she asked.

"Never. I've heard plenty about it from Jack, but I hate to say I never spent much time past the overpass when I lived here."

That was a common townie saying. It was one that applied equally to Ginny.

147

"Where'd you go to school?"

"I'm a Brother Rice boy."

"Before or after they went co-ed?"

"How old do you think I am? Trust me, there were plenty of girls in my graduating class. How about you?"

"Bishop's."

"Ah, not a good Catholic girl, then?"

"I'm not as old as you think I am," she said with a laugh. "I graduated after the end of denominational schools."

She pulled up the steep driveway of the inn. It had a liberal helping of salt layered on top, keeping it not completely free of snow, but not as slippery as the road through town.

There were two spots left in the parking lot. A pit opened in her stomach. She wasn't going to get to stay here unless she took Sean's room.

"No point bringing in any luggage till we know what's going on," he said, hopping out of the car the second she put it in park. In a flash he was on her side of the car, opening the door.

He did the same a second later when they made their way to the huge double oak doors of the inn.

"Buddy," a happy voice shouted out as they stepped inside. "'Bout time you came to see me." Sean disappeared in a hug by a bear of a man.

Not just any man. One of Ginny's guilty pleasures was hockey. Jack Walsh was one of the best players to ever play in the National Hockey League, and he was from Newfoundland. She wasn't up on all the details, but she recalled he'd been hurt a couple of years ago and had retired. She'd had no idea he had come back home.

While it would have suited her fine to eavesdrop on their conversation—what chance would she have to be this close to a hockey god again?—a tall brunette approached.

"You managed to beat the snow," she said, her voice beautifully laced with a Scottish accent. "I'm Daphne. I'm working on getting you a place to stay . . . but I don't think it's going to be here."

Ginny's heart dropped. So much for a night of luxurious pampering.

"Oh, no, don't be sad," the woman said, shaking her head emphatically. "There's nothing to worry about at all. These things have a way of working themselves out. Worse comes to worst, we've a couple of guest rooms in our house you're welcome to." She lowered her voice. "I don't meant to pry, but you really won't be sharing a bed with Sean? Sometimes guests like separate rooms, even though . . ."

Words failed her. Some sort of stammering noise came forth that was garbled and breathy.

Daphne wrapped her arm around Ginny's shoulder and led her away. "Okay. Separate beds. Got it. While I'm trying to sort this out, feel free to explore. The dining room is straight through here," she said, still guiding Ginny along. A quick glance at a warm and inviting buttercream room with fine linens and china, not to mention full of people enjoying some tantalizing-smelling foods, was all she got before being led along the hall.

"This is the library. Nice and quiet. And warm. The games room." Daphne pointed to another room. "Well, I'd avoid that right now. There's quite a high-stakes game of a hundred and twenties going on. Basically, this whole floor is full of spots to relax. There's a couple of guest rooms on this floor, but they're tucked out of the way."

"Have you worked here long?" Ginny thought the woman was the perfect hostess and loved to give staff compliments when well-deserved.

Daphne laughed. "I don't work here at all. But Elsie, my sister-in-law, is beyond busy, so I thought I'd lend a hand. I love it in Heart's Ease, but I need to get out of the house sometimes. And there's always something interesting happening over here."

Ginny wanted to ask if there were any famous guests staying there but bit her tongue. The place had a reputation for random sightings of actors and rock stars. There were even rumours of a royal visit.

Thoughts of a handsome prince were wiped away with the scent of Sean. It was weird she recognized his cologne, but she'd spent a couple of hours in the car with him. The man smelled damn good. She didn't think she'd ever forget it.

"Are you sick of my company yet? Or can I entice you to have supper with me while these two figure out where we're sleeping tonight?"

"Don't you have a room?" Damn, she wished the spark of excitement that sizzled to life in her stomach—okay, truth be told, lower than her stomach—would stop burning whenever the notion of Sean and a bed came to mind.

She wasn't this girl. She didn't get swoony or horny over a man she'd known for a grand total of maybe three hours.

Or at least she hadn't been. There was no denying the tingles in her body that had roared to life this morning and had only gotten stronger.

Thinking back on her conversation with Laura earlier, this was clearly her gut giving her an overwhelming feeling. But would she do anything about it? Could she?

Daphne shrugged and gave a sheepish grimace. "Jack told Elsie it would be okay to give away Sean's room tonight. The guest who was supposed to check out today heard about the snow and wanted to stay and see it. We figured Sean could crash at our place. I figured he and Jack would be up half the night anyhow and didn't think it would matter. Sorry."

"I'm not upset," Sean said, smiling in reassurance. "I'd thought I'd give Ginny my room is all."

It was fine and dandy for him. He had a place to sleep.

"Don't worry. Like I said, we'll figure it all out. Now go have yourself something to eat so I can get you a couple of beds." Daphne laid a hand on Ginny's arm. "A couple of rooms," she said with a smile.

"I don't mind sharing a room if Ginny doesn't mind."

Her legs weakened at his words. And then nearly collapsed when he stroked the top of her shoulder. "No pressure," he said more quietly. "Whatever you're comfortable with. I'll be a total gentleman."

The good-girl portion of her brain railed against the very idea.

The girl-who-wasn't-sure-who-she-wanted-to-be portion thought something very different. That often-shushed voice, amazed to have an attentive ear, proclaimed other women acted on their desires and gladly told the tale after.

Somewhere in her mind her mother's voice threatened to come to life, but Ginny quickly shut that down. Her mother was on a plane far from here. All judgment was gone.

She smiled at Sean. "I've no doubt. I think we could manage in one room if need be."

His eyes narrowed, and she swore there was a glimmer of surprise there. What reason did he have to look so shocked? He barely knew her. Couldn't know of her history of shying away from anything she'd have to lie to her mother about.

Then that glimmer grew brighter, and she wondered if perhaps it wasn't disbelief as much as interest.

No way. There was no way he was having palpitations in his naughty bits over her. Was there?

"See? We're troopers," he told Daphne before looping his arm through Ginny's. "When there's a white Christmas on the horizon, there's no point letting a little old thing like modesty ruin it." Turning away from Jack and Daphne, he led her back down the wide hallway to the delicious scents of cinnamon and apples wafting out of the dining room.

"Regretting helping me out?" Sean asked as he pulled a chair out for Ginny.

"Not in the least. If I were home I'd be eating instant noodles and getting ready . . ."

Too much information. She cut herself off before confessing she was going to a party where she'd spend the night drinking herself into pity. Sean didn't know how pathetic her life was. And whatever paltry attraction he seemed to have for her wouldn't be improved on if she revealed how lame she was.

"Well, I was going to a party. But I do that every year. It's nice to be somewhere different this year. It's a good start to my first Christmas alone."

Sean's face grew serious. "You're alone for the holidays?"

She shrugged. "By choice. My brother flew my mom down to his place today. That's why I was at the airport. I could have gone but, honestly, I could use a break from the expected. It's nice to have a bit of unpredictability in my life for a change."

"I'd say nearly getting beheaded by an escalator is pretty unpredictable."

"Being rescued by a—by you—was pretty unexpected, too."

"By a me?" He laughed. God, he laughed a lot. It was refreshing. "What am I? A species of my own?" He paused. Stopped laughing and stared at her. "You're blushing."

Of course she was blushing. Even if he sat there and said nothing, the way his eyes slowly roamed across her face, and a little lower, sent a heat through her. She'd never been seduced. Had no idea if that was what was happening. But one thing was for certain. A man had never gazed at her as if she were worth considering.

To hell with it. She'd never see him again after today. Or maybe tomorrow. What did she have to lose in flirting a little? In stepping out of her shell?

"I'm not sure species is the correct word. That would mean there'd have to be more than one. And God help the women of the world if there's a roving band of men who look like you out there."

Ha. He blushed. She'd made a man blush. Laura would be proud of her.

"So one of me is enough, then?"

"Prodding for more compliments?"

"Just fact checking."

"Check a mirror. That should make it clear."

Again with the laughter.

"You're fast with the comebacks this evening. Talking to you in the car was a little one-sided. I was thinking you didn't like me."

"I was making up my mind. It was touch and go there for a while with all the speed-demon chatter."

"So what changed your mind?"

She took a drink of water and caught the eye of a server. Time to bring the conversation to a halt.

"Oh, no, you're not getting away that easy," he said, wagging a finger. "We'll be revisiting this topic as soon as you answer one very critical question. And think carefully. My entire opinion of you hangs in the balance."

Her stomach flipped.

"Red or white?"

"Wine?"

"Yes, wine. What's your choice?"

"Red," she said without hesitation. "Red in winter, white in summer."

"Beer in summer," he said before turning to the waiter. "A bottle of—" he faced her again. "Do you like Malbec or would you prefer something else?"

"That's perfect," she said, thinking about an entire bottle of wine coming to the table. Clearly he didn't have a fast dinner in mind.

This was made doubly clear by the amount of food he ordered. The man couldn't make up his mind what he wanted to try, and so a helping of everything was en route.

"It's been a while since I've seen a menu this filled with real food. Seriously. You think I've ever seen salt beef or scruncheons on a menu in New York?"

"You live in New York?" She'd assumed he lived in Toronto or Montreal. Maybe Vancouver. New York City just took it to a whole other level.

"Not in the city. But it's drivable. I'm between permanent gigs right now, so I'm floating around the east coast working with different teams, seeing what feels right. For a long time I worked with Jack when he was still in the NHL. When he left the team, it wasn't as fun anymore. Last year I dabbled in football, but it's not my sport."

"There's that much work for a sports physiotherapist?"

This was a world she knew nothing about. Her only encounter with physio was years ago when she'd broken her leg helping Daniel move. He still gave her a hard time about breaking his PlayStation.

No! Thoughts of Daniel were not welcome tonight. Dear God, please let Sean King conduct a successful exorcism.

She tried to get him to expand on his work, but he wasn't interested.

"If all we have to talk about is work, this is going to be a dull evening. I'm much more interested in you. I'm trying to understand why a beautiful woman would pass up a party to drive a stranger to one of the most romantic destinations on the island. You're going to have to help me rein in my overactive imagination. Or not."

Those eyes of his were alight with mischief. It was hard to interpret them. Was he playing? Was he serious? Was this simple flirtation or something more?

Sweet Santa, let him not be playing. Ginny had made up her mind. If this man offered more to her tonight than dinner, she was taking it. It was the universe's gift to her.

Picking up her glass of wine, she gulped some courage.

"I'm not spontaneous," she said, taking another large sip. "I rarely step out of my routine. Nothing ever comes my way to make me consider trying something new. And I'm tired of regrets. If I'd let you walk out of the shop today, I would have spent tonight wondering what had happened to you. I certainly would have kicked myself for not offering you a ride." There was more she wanted to say, but another sip of wine was needed to make it happen.

"So you're telling me you drove two hours to be a good Samaritan? Nothing more?"

"I drove two hours because I wasn't sure what I wanted."

"And the drive? Did it help? Those two hours? Do you know what you want now?"

When had he leaned across the table? How was it possible he was taking up so much space?

She reached for her glass again, but he covered the top of it with his hand.

"Oh, no. I don't want liquid courage. I don't want what could happen tonight to be fuelled by booze. I want you thinking with a clear head. I want you to make up your mind now about what you want. Then you can drink to your heart's content. But if something happens between us tonight, I damn well want you to remember it."

She couldn't breathe. His eyes penetrated hers, questioning.

"You're not spontaneous? Neither am I. And I'm not reckless. Not when it comes to women." He let his hand slip from covering the wine glass to cover her own. The touch of his skin on hers made her shift in her seat. That subtle move nearly drove her to run.

"I don't go around seducing strangers. Ask Jack. That's not my style."

"Then why now? Why me?"

There was no point denying it. His intentions were clear. He wanted her. For some unknown reason, but there it was.

VICTORIA BARBOUR

He leaned back in his chair and smiled. "I was waiting all day to see if this was an act. But it's not. You truly don't remember."

Her heart lurched. "Remember what?" Her voice was barely a whisper.

"Remember kissing me."

"I kissed you? Are you crazy?" What kind of a question was that? He clearly was.

"You certainly did."

"When?"

"Two years ago. Paddy's Day weekend in Boston."

Shit. Shit. Shit. Was he right? She was in Boston two years ago with Laura and a few more friends. There'd been a lot of drinking. Too much drinking. But she had no recollection of Sean. Nothing. If they'd kissed, she'd remember it, wouldn't she?

"You're trying to remember, aren't you? Would it help if I told you that you were incredibly drunk? Although to your credit, you can hold your liquor. I didn't realize how drunk you were at first."

"Oh Jesus," she said, hiding her hands in her face, "I'm mortified."

"Don't be. I'm not telling you this to embarrass you. You didn't do anything at all to make a fool of yourself. Unless you consider kissing me foolish." He shrugged. "Which is always possible."

She shook her head. "I don't remember at all! That's it." She pushed her wineglass away. "I'm not drinking any more."

Then she grabbed it back. "Screw that." She took a swig. "Tell me, please. What happened?"

"Let me see if I can help you. What's your favourite TV show?"

"Favourite? I don't have a favourite. I watch a lot of shows."

"But you like *Grey's Anatomy*?"

"I did. I've quit." She took a good hard look at him. And a haze seemed to lift.

"Oh God. The elevator."

"You do remember."

"I don't remember it. Not really. But I remember a dream." She raked her hand over her face and exhaled. In for a penny, in for a pound. "It's sort of a recurring dream."

"Tell me your dream."

"No way. I'm already mortified. I want the truth."

He topped up her wine and gave her the kindest smile she'd ever received.

"First of all, there is no reason to be mortified. That kiss, that moment, is nothing to be ashamed of. It was fun. And memorable."

She snorted. "Glad it was memorable for one of us."

"Yeah, if anyone should feel bad, it's me. Here I am with this memory of one of the best kisses of my life and you don't even remember me."

"Tell me what happened."

"It was late, well after midnight. I was down in the basement of the hotel in the fitness centre working off some steam.

It was a hard game that night, and I'd fought with the coaches after they told one of the guys to get back on the ice even though I'd said he needed to sit out the rest of the game. Anyway, I was in the elevator, when it stopped on the main floor. The most incredible woman was standing there. Long wavy honey gold hair, natural, not primped and smoothed to an inch of its life. Stunning brown eyes. And a sweet round face that was warm and kind. Even with a smudged green shamrock on her cheek."

Ginny's breath caught. She wasn't beautiful. Certainly not incredible. Her mother often told her she was pretty when she bothered to do her hair and makeup. Sean was clearly trying to spare her feelings.

"Do you know what you said when the elevator opened?"

"I don't want to know."

"You looked me up and down and then turned to an older guy who was waiting to get on with you and said, 'You better take the next one. I need some time alone with McDreamy here.'"

"That's how you knew about *Grey's Anatomy*." With a groan she grabbed a slice of bread and stuffed it into her mouth.

"He smiled and walked away and you sauntered in. You were very cute. And sexy."

I can imagine, she thought.

"So then I got on and assaulted you?"

"Of course not. Do I seem like a helpless man to you?"

He paused and took a spoonful of the chowder that was laid in front of him.

"You got on and were as quiet as a mouse. You must have thought I didn't hear what you said. We went up three or four floors, and all was silent. That's when I pointed out to you that you hadn't pressed a button. You looked at the number seventeen glowing and said, 'That's my floor.' I thought it was funny that we were on the same floor, but I didn't realize how drunk you were. I knew you were tipsy, though. We stood there, silent, for the whole way up. Until the door opened and you turned to me and said, 'Thank you for a lovely night. This might be the best date I've never had.' And then you kissed me. Kissed me and walked off the elevator. I was shocked. The door closed and I just stood there, forgetting for a second I'd missed my floor. Then the door opened and you got back on. 'I'm on the seventh floor.' You held the door for me, and I stepped off. And never saw you again. Until this morning at the airport."

"Is that why you knocked into me?"

"No. That was an accident. It was when I turned and saw you. Imagine my shock finding my mystery Boston woman here at home. I thought I was losing my mind at first. But I didn't get to say anything because of what happened. And the whole time I'm talking to you, I can tell you don't recognize me. Or if you do, you were doing a great job of pretending not to know me."

His mystery Boston woman? That's how he'd been thinking of her. For two years. This man. This ripped from the pages of world's hottest man weekly.

"You have to believe me," she said. "I have no recollection of any of that. And I'm so sorry. Why weren't you embarrassed?"

"I'm a man. Embarrassment isn't quite the feeling that overcomes me when a smokin' hot lady checks me out and then kisses me. It took all I had that night not to go looking for you."

"Why didn't you?"

"Because I knew. I felt it in my gut that this wasn't who you were. That it was booze and not reality. And I've never taken pride in drunken conquests. It's not me."

God. Did he think she was a lush?

"That's not normal for me," she said, hoping he could tell how sincere she was. "Getting drunk and hitting on guys. That's not my thing." She picked up her glass of water and drank deep. "Trust me. When I tell my friends—if I tell my friends—about this, they'll never believe me."

"I believe you."

Her shoulders relaxed a little. Even her breath became stronger. She could even contemplate eating now without fear of simultaneously choking on her food and puking.

The rest of dinner was quiet. Comfortably quiet with a few comments here and there on the quality of the food—stupendous—and the snow outside—serene. Sean didn't mention Boston again. Ginny didn't ask any of the multitude of questions rolling around in her brain. Partly because she didn't know how to ask them. And also because she wasn't sure if she wanted the answer.

Truth be told, she enjoyed the way Sean stole a glance at

her from time to time. Or the way he refilled her water glass. She hadn't touched her wine for the rest of the meal. One thing he'd said made sense. Whatever decision she made tonight, she was doing it with a clear head.

By the time Daphne came to the table, all the discomfort was gone. Ginny appreciated a man who didn't need to fill a peaceful silence with empty chatter.

"Well, kids," Daphne said. "I come bearing good news. A room has made itself available after all. We had a last-minute cancellation because of the weather. So, Sean, you can crash at our place. And, Ginny, you get a beautiful room all to yourself. If you give me your keys, I'll get your luggage brought up to your room."

"I can bring your suitcase up if you like," Sean said, a questioning glimmer in his eyes.

"Yes, please," Ginny said, her voice barely a whisper. She wasn't ready to let him go yet. The threat of having to share a room had become a promise she was sorry to see broken.

Daphne dropped the key on the table and smiled at Ginny. It was the smile all women recognized, maybe because of how infrequent it was. A good-for-you kind of smile that held no judgment.

"The house is only a short walk down the lane," she told Sean. "We'll leave the door open."

FOUR

The room was breathtaking. Shades of blush pink and soft creams in all manner of matte fabrics created an oasis of warmth. It was subtly decorated for Christmas with sparse hints of evergreen on the mantel of a crackling fireplace that reminded Ginny of a Christmas card. Tall windows gave a postcard view of the snow that was falling gently, a far better sight than the usual squalls. In a corner that stretched to soaring heights for a historic manor house stood a tall, slim spruce softly lit with white lights, and white, gold, and red glass bulbs. Ginny couldn't believe this was where she was spending the night. This room was beyond perfect. It was the living incarnation of what she'd do with her own bedroom if she had the imagination and means to make it happen.

She closed the door behind her and laid her jacket on the alabaster crushed velvet loveseat that faced the fire. Sean wasn't back from the car yet. It gave her a moment to herself. Stretching her arms wide, she twirled around the room until she made herself giddy. This day was unlike any other. When tomorrow came and the spell was broken, when Ginny Winter went back to being invisible, the kind of girl who listened in rapt attention to other people's too-good-to-be-true tales instead of the one who told the tales, well, she'd always have the memories she was making right now.

Kicking off her boots, she leaped onto the huge four-post bed and pulled out her cellphone. A selfie to prove this was real would be necessary at some point in her life.

Big mistake. Leave it to technology to remind her of real life. Several texts from Daniel wondering if she could pick up food, go to the liquor store, and "swing by and pick up Brittney" on her way. Who the hell was Brittney? It didn't matter. None of it mattered. One day with Sean had helped show her she didn't need Daniel. For too long she'd been subservient to him. First hoping he'd notice her as more than a friend. Then praying he'd realize how good they were together. And finally, most pathetically, wishing he'd see the error of his ways and come back.

No more. She was done with that.

In a pique she sent him her selfie with a quick note: Sorry I'm missing the party. Sean took me out for the night. If I don't see you before Christmas, have a merry one.

God, that felt good. The immediate text back was even better.

Who's Sean?

Miraculously, the need to try to make Daniel jealous disappeared. It didn't matter. She didn't want him jealous. She wanted him to realize that she had her own life beyond his world.

Turning off her phone, she tossed it on the night table and smiled. Even if all she did for the rest of the night was curl up in this bed and read a book, it would still be one of the best nights of her life.

A soft knock on the door made her jump. Here was the potential for an even more amazing night. She rushed across the room and pulled it open.

Sean's hair was damp from the snow, and a few fat, fluffy flakes were still intact on his jacket.

"It looks nice out," he said, setting down her bag, "but it's really coming down."

"You don't have to rush off to Jack's right away. Wait for the snow to lighten up."

Ginny was impressed she didn't say any of that as a question.

"I wasn't planning on rushing off," he said, kicking the door closed behind him and wrapping his arms around her waist.

Her body tensed. This was what she wanted. But she'd thought he'd ease into it.

Whether it was the soft light in the room or her imagination, she was certain his eyes were darker, more intense than before. He reached up and brushed her hair back from her face.

"Breathe," he said, his voice deep. "I'm not going to kiss you."

"Forgive me for thinking that's not true."

She felt his laugh before she heard it, low and sensual, as if laughing were part of the pleasure.

"Oh, we're going to kiss." His lips were so close to hers she could feel the slight shift of air between them. "But you're going to kiss me."

Her body tensed further. That was too much pressure.

"Don't," he said, pulling her closer. "Don't pull away. I'm still not sure if this is real, that I'm not having some out-of-body Christmas experience, getting what I've wished for. Do you know how many nights I've laid awake trying to remember the feel of your lips on mine? Kicking myself for not following you?"

"You have?" She licked her lips and swallowed.

"I have."

It was an incredible thing to witness a man search her face, as if drinking in her features. For the first time in her life, Ginny felt desired. And she felt it right to the very core of her body. Hot. Cold. Anxious. Powerful. So many feelings at once.

Tentatively, she brought her hand up his back, resting the base of her hand on his neck, letting her fingers glide through his short silken hair.

His eyes fluttered closed as he drew in a sharp breath. Amazing. She was causing this. Her.

"Open your eyes, Sean," she said, marvelling at the sensual rasp in her voice. "If you want me to kiss you, open your eyes."

Instantly, two pools of steel blue bore into hers. All it took was an instant, and she lightly brushed her lips against his. Pulled back. Wondered how she'd kissed him that night. Stopped caring. Forget the past. She knew exactly how she wanted to kiss him right now.

Pulling his mouth to hers, she opened her lips enough to taste his bottom lip, then his top. Then she stopped thinking at all, revelling in the kiss, in the way he responded. He was taller than she was but not uncomfortably so. No. He was perfectly taller than she was. Their mouths were meant to fit each other.

With a quick turn, he walked her toward the door, pressing her against the heavy oak. When she tried to slip her hand up his shirt, he tangled his fingers in hers and held them against the door.

"Not yet," he rasped before prying her mouth open more, tasting her with a need she gladly matched.

Never had a kiss left her body yearning, burning, begging for more. Not like this. Some powerful nymph had awakened in her, starving for a touch only one man could deliver. A soft guttural moan escaped from her mouth. Instead of shame, she was awash with a sense of sensuality.

Sean dropped her hands and scooped her into his arms, carrying her across the room. But instead of bringing her to the bed, he lowered her onto the small sofa, pulling her onto his lap. Not once did their lips part. His hands moved from her waist to her hair, knotting one fist in her hair before sending her into near oblivion when he slid his other hand over her shirt to caress her breast.

"You're incredible," he ground out.

"You make me incredible," she said, shocked by the boldness of her words. "Only for you."

With a groan, he pulled away.

"Ginny. I want you." Tracing her lips with his finger, he kissed her softly. "I want you more than I've ever wanted anything in my life."

Her eyes grew heavy with desire. "I want you," she said. "I know it's just one night. But, God, I don't care. I'm yours tonight. Whatever you want."

"Jesus," he said, running a hand through his hair. "This is ridiculous."

Her face fell. Ridiculous?

"Not you," he said, kissing her again. "This situation. I don't want to have tonight with you and nothing more. I've dreamed about you for too long to have you disappear again in the morning." He stood. Walked across the room and poured a glass of water. "I can't explain this without sounding . . ."

He paced. Ginny sat still, watching in amazement.

"I don't have sex with strangers. I don't do it. It was a rule I made for myself when I started travelling with my first hockey team. Watching guys hop in and out of bed with a different woman in every town. It wasn't for me. After my mother passed away, Dad came to spend a week with me. His kidneys were already failing, and I knew it was likely his last trip. We talked a lot, and he asked about women. I was between girlfriends, and he assumed I was having a wild time.

When I told him my rule, God, Ginny, the look of pride on his face left me speechless."

Her heart ached for him. For this man who was right. They were strangers. She didn't even know his parents were dead. It explained why he was alone at Christmas.

"It's okay," she said, meaning it. "I understand."

"I want you to stay," he said. "Stay here in Heart's Ease for Christmas. I want to get to know you. I want to kiss you again. And damn it all, I want you. But I want to know you better first. I don't want our first time together to be a frenzy of me acting out on a fantasy of a memory. I want to be with you."

"I'm not that interesting," she said, hating the sheepish tone of her voice. "This version of me, it's not real."

"I beg to differ. Everything I've experienced with you so far is pretty damn real and interesting. Don't sell yourself short."

"I don't know," she said. Her mind was a torrent of twisty thoughts. What was waiting for her back in St. John's? An orchid, a cat, and a friend who'd give her a kick in the arse if she let this opportunity pass her by.

"Is it the cost of the room? I was renting a room anyway. I can pay for it. We can go halfs. Whatever makes you comfortable. Hell, come stay at Jack's. He won't care. Just stay. We'll figure it out."

She tried to find a good reason to say no.

"The thought of you alone for Christmas will ruin my holiday. You don't want that, do you?"

She laughed. "Are you trying to guilt me into it?"

"I think I'm desperate," he said. "I guess I'll try anything."

She closed her eyes. Thought about her next words. Opened them again.

"I'll stay. And I'll hold you to your word. You'll know so much about me that you'll go running for the hills. But you'll know me. And we'll start right now. Hand me my bag," she said, not moving from the chair.

He nearly sprang across the room.

"I'm boring," she told him, pulling out a roll of soft cotton and her crochet hook. "A normal night for me isn't making out with a candidate for *People*'s most sexy list. It's watching TV, drinking tea, and crocheting. Think you can spend an hour with me doing just that?"

"I think I can spend a long, long time doing just that," he said, sitting next to her and turning on the TV. He propped his feet on the little table in front of the fire. "Under one condition."

"What's that?"

"You kiss me during every commercial break."

Ginny's heart soared. She didn't believe in perfect. And tomorrow she might wake up and realize she'd made one hell of a mistake. But right now, it all seemed perfect. It was worth taking a chance.

The TV flickered to life. A bright loud advertisement for lotto tickets blared from the speakers.

"Sean," she said, dropping her crochet hook and pulling him toward her. "It's going to be a long night."

"God, I hope so," he replied.
And indeed it was.

Welcome to Heart's Ease

Thanks for reading! If this is your first time reading anything by me, I wanted to tell you a little about the setting for my Heart's Ease stories.

Heart's Ease is a fictional community in my home province of Newfoundland and Labrador. It's nestled around a small harbour in Trinity Bay (the Heart's Content side, not the Trinity side). A lot of people ask me if it's real. It's not. Although there is a Little Heart's Ease on the Trinity side, and I believe there once was a Heart's Ease near that as well. I created Heart's Ease and the people who call it home to show what it is to live in a small fishing community on the edge of North America. I love where I live, and I love the people who I meet here. For me, Heart's Ease is a love letter to my home.

The stories I tell about Heart's Ease tend to be light and happy. Why? Because there's enough doom and gloom in the world. Heart's Ease is a place to escape and feel better. And I hope that, after reading any of the stories set here, you feel the same. I know I do when I'm writing them.

If you'd like to show your appreciation, reviews are always the best way to help an author you like. Did you know that our sales and advertising opportunities are often determined by the number of reviews we have?

If you've enjoyed this book, I would love it if you could pop over to Amazon, Kobo, iBooks, or wherever you read, and leave a review. I think they'll even prompt you for one at the end of this book. It really is the best way to show an author you like their work. Don't do it just for me! Leave a review for any book you enjoy. It doesn't even have to be long. A simple "I liked it" or "I'd recommend this book" does the trick.

Finally, if you'd like to keep up to date on new releases, why not take a second and sign up for my mailing list? People who sign up get exclusive content. You can expect in the future to receive access to other exclusive stories. I'll let you know when they are available through email.

As always, you have my promise not to spam you. I will only send emails when I have a new release or news to share.

In the following pages you'll find descriptions of all my Heart's Ease books. If you'd like to take a virtual trip there, just click the link for the book. And as always, if you enjoy what you read, I'd really appreciate a review when you've finished.

∾

Against Her Rules

Elsie Walsh had it all. Or so she thought. Until Scottish hunk Campbell Scott showed up on the doorstep of her bed and breakfast. He's making it pretty hard for her to stand by her one rule: No sleeping with the guests. She's denied some of the world's hottest actors, musicians, and even royals . . . but how can she keep Cam out of her bed, when he's invaded her head and her heart?

Campbell Scott went to the wilds of Newfoundland with one thing on his mind: sketch some birds, and then get back to his playboy lifestyle in London. But one look at his sexy hostess and there's a whole lot more in the air than seabirds. Rejection isn't part of his vocabulary, and Cam sets out to not only convince Elsie that he belongs in her bed, but by her side at the Heart's Ease Inn.

Hard as Ice

The first time Daphne Scott met hunky hockey superstar Jack Walsh, she was hungover and more than a little irritable. Still, it was hard to deny that he was hotter than Adonis—even if he did know it.

The second time Jack met the sexy Scottish beauty Daphne, he had a concussion and wanted nothing more than to get home to Heart's Ease so he could recover. He didn't expect the ice queen to become his best medicine.

A whirlwind romance at the Heart's Ease Inn seems like

the best prescription for them both. Until the real world creeps in, forcing them to learn that making a long-distance relationship work is harder than either imagined. When their careers threaten to put half a world between them, they must make a choice. Have they taken on a task harder than the very ice he skates on?

Play Me

When sparks fly between sultry lawyer Fiona Nolan and sexy folksinger Dillon O'Dea, little do they know that they're about to turn a long simmering family feud into an all-out scorcher.

From the moment she sets eyes on Dillon, Fiona knows that she's willing to play for keeps, even if it means upsetting her family. And when she takes on a case to defend one of her family's enemies, will Heart's Ease ever be the same idyllic escape?

Together, Dillon and Fiona fight back against one of the oldest conflicts in Heart's Ease history, relying on the power of family and music to bring harmony back to the town.

21st Century Rake

Rock superstar Asher Corbin is back in Heart's Ease. And he's not alone. This time he's brought the entire cast and crew for his upcoming film debut to the small town for a retreat back in time to the Regency period.

Grace Nolan is thrilled to go to an honest-to-goodness Regency ball. But there she finds herself at the mercy of her deepest fantasy: a scandalous rake fresh out of the pages of her favourite historical romances.

When Grace claims not to recognize the dashing celebrity, Asher seizes the opportunity to step out of his persona and explore life out of the spotlight. But when she finds out his secret, her response plunges them into a game of seduction neither had expected to find.

Wilful Desire

Will Walsh is a terrific sailor. And a terrible ex. Just ask Mae Mercer, the woman he left behind when a too-good-to-refuse promotion to the elite ranks of the Navy came on the eve of their wedding.

Will might be a force of nature when he's hunting down pirates and drug dealers, but that's nothing compared to the way he capsizes Mae's world when he returns home to Heart's Ease. On a mission to reclaim her heart, he knows that failure isn't an option. But this time, he might have to concede defeat: the only thing stronger than his desire to claim her is Mae's desire to preserve her freedom.

Can Mae resist the temptation to jump into this very able-bodied seaman's open arms? Or will his wilful desire win out?

If you love clean and wholesome romance . . .

Don't miss Victoria Barbour's new series:

The Honky-Tonk Bridal Shop

Inspired by TLC's *Say Yes to the Dress,* classic country crooners, and sweet, modern western romances.

Sign up for Victoria's Honky-Tonk Bridal Shop emails and be among the first to get a sneak-peek of her upcoming new series.

ACKNOWLEDGEMENTS

Phew. What a learning experience this book has been. Taking a novella and turning it into a longer book is harder than I imagined. And just like the first version of *Christmas in the Harbour*, this newly expanded version wouldn't have made it to the end without a lot of helping words of encouragement. As always, my partner in life and love, Reg Stoyles, made finishing another book possible. Thanks my love for the support you never fail to give, in my writing and in all things. A huge thanks to Melanie Martin and Libby Creelman, who stepped up at the end and helped me get over the finish line. And thanks again to my amazing cover designer, Crystal McLellan, for putting a touch of winter magic on this one. Finally, thank you so much to everyone at Flanker Press, but especially Garry, Margo, and Jerry Cranford. It was Garry who convinced me to expand the story so Flanker Press could bring it to my wonderful print book readers. Which brings me to the biggest thank you of all. Thank YOU! Yes, you. I'm truly amazed and honoured every time readers like you take the time to read the stories I create.

I write my stories to entertain myself, and you. And if your feedback is anything to go by, I'm doing okay. I read every review, email, and message you write, even if I don't always respond quickly. Trust me when I say that there are days when I don't feel like writing. But I check my email or Facebook and there's always someone there to remind me of why I write. Thank you!

 A *USA TODAY* bestselling author, Victoria Barbour lives on the island of Newfoundland, and is fiercely proud of her home. She can imagine no better setting for her works, and hopes that her readers will one day come to witness Newfoundland and Labrador's rustic beauty for themselves.

Victoria was born in St. John's and raised above her family's fish and chips restaurant. She has travelled and lived in other parts of Canada but chose to make her home where her heart has long resided. Victoria has a degree in history from Memorial University of Newfoundland, with a minor in Newfoundland studies. The only thing that stands between her and a master's degree in history from Simon Fraser University in British Columbia is her thesis. She has a background in broadcast journalism, advertising, and marketing. She is a proud member of several writing organizations, including the Romance Writers of America (RWA); their affiliate chapter, Romance Writers of Atlantic Canada (RWAC); Romancing the Rock, and the Writers' Alliance of Newfoundland and Labrador (WANL).

Victoria counts herself lucky to be surrounded by an incredibly supportive family. She thanks her husband daily for his unerring faith in her and for being a wonderful father to their energetic but always entertaining son.